The Garden
in Which
I Walk

The Garden in Which I Walk

BY KAREN BRENNAN

FC2
NORMAL/TALLAHASSEE

Published by FC2 with support provided by Florida State University, the
Publications Unit of the Department of English at Illinois State Univer-
sity, the Illinois Arts Council, and the Florida Arts Council of the Florida
Division of Cultural Affairs.

Address all inquiries to: Fiction Collective Two, Florida State University,
c/o English Department, Tallahassee, FL 32306-1580

ISBN: Paper, 1-57366-116-3

Library of Congress Cataloging-in-Publication Data
Brennan, Karen, 1941-
  The garden in which I walk / by Karen Brennan.— 1st ed.
    p. cm.
  ISBN 1-57366-116-3
  1. United States—Social life and customs—Fiction. I. Title.
  PS3552.R378G37 2004
  813'.54—dc22
                                        2004004924

Cover Design: Lou Robinson
Book Design: Brooke Nelson and Tara Reeser

Produced and printed in the United States of America.
Printed on recycled paper with soy ink.

ACKNOWLEDGEMENTS

"The Garden in Which I Walk"   *VOLT*

"Three Seaside Tales"   *Ploughshares*

"Secret Encounters"   *Global City Review*

"Saw"   *Great Harvest Anthology*

"The Emergence of Modernism"   *TriQuarterly*

"Happy Girl"   *TriQuarterly*

"Paradise"   *Chimera*

"Island Time"   *Bellingham Review*

"On Vision"   *Fiction International*

"The Soul in its Flight"   *Western Humanities Review*

To my students

Meanwhile the mind, from pleasure less,
Withdraws into its happiness:
The mind, that ocean where each kind
Does straight its own resemblance find,
Yet it creates, transcending these,
Far other worlds, and other seas,
Annihilating all that's made
To a green thought in a green shade.

ANDREW MARVELL

Deep down, all the while, she was waiting for something
to happen.

GUSTAVE FLAUBERT

CONTENTS

THE GARDEN
IN WHICH
I WALK

is in the shadow of the forty-story Church office building. There are peonies, white, pink, mauve. There are delphiniums, daisies, bamboo grass, chicken-and-egg, coleus of all colors, forget-me-nots, tiny violas with yellow centers. There are sprinklers which mist even the concrete. There is brownish concrete when wet, otherwise grey. There is a fountain where water shoots out like a waterfall into an enormous granite bowl. There is a statue of a handsome religious leader holding hands with and looking into the eyes of his dear wife. There are accompanying bronzes of children dancing in a circle, very joyous. There is a slight breeze. There is a man pushing his bicycle along, pushing it along gravely, but seemingly without destination. There are sprinklers which mist even the man's bicycle as he traverses the narrow walkways. There is a sharp squeaky sound coming from a nearby traffic light which reminds me of a car burglar alarm. There are no burglars. There are no people coming into or going out of the forty-story office building (it's Sunday). There's me walking along in my new black shoes (avoiding therefore the misting sprinklers) and my black hat. There is the man with his bicycle who is now going in the opposite direction from the first direction in which he had been headed. There are no bugs discernible to the naked eyeball, there is a bigger breeze, there is the black hat tilted, blown askew by the breeze which has now the force of a wind. There are fat mounds of dirt beneath each clump of flowers. There are no weeds, no errant plant growths, no unruly anthills marring these dirt mounds. There are mountains in the distance which have jagged peaks like the mountains of Switzerland. There is snow on some of the mountains even though it is August. There is a moderate amount of religious fervor in the air. There are cars speeding by which are visible over the ridge of the waterfall-like fountain. There are minuscule chips of stone embedded in the concrete over which the fountain water flows. There is a shadow on the garden from the office building, an actual shadow from the forty-story office building, and a figurative shadow, call it historical. There is a man who is now pausing with his bicycle, staring idly at the Lady Banks roses. There is a certain kind of comfort being offered here, that is to say a certain precious, adorable kind of comfort that invites you to surrender everything in return for a nice vanilla cream pie. There are no pies. There is instead a profusion of flowers everywhere in this garden in their perfectly manicured, well-maintained beds, growing as per arrangement, according to plan with no weeds. There is everywhere the grim overhang of the office building, but then there is also the sky which is a pale cloudless blue, and the breeze which accelerated into wind and now is stronger wind, and the mountains with their little jagged frozen snow caps. There is me running after my hat, which is dipping and soaring with a mind of its own into the fountain bowl where it fills with water and sinks. There is the bicycle man alerted by the clomp-clomp of my shoes on the pavement and veering his bicycle toward where I am running after my hat. There I am sitting by the side of the fountain, my arm submerged to the elbow trying for the hat and swearing loudly with no fear of offending anyone, having momentarily forgotten about the man with the bicycle who is now unmistakably moving toward me, pushing his bicycle which has a creaky wheel. There is the wind dying down. There is a penny in a crack between blocks of grey aggregate. There is me gazing intently at the penny because there is the man heading toward me, coming closer. There is the man offering to retrieve my hat. There is the man with his arm submerged to the elbow in fountain water. There is a moustache on the man, speckled with white at the very ends as if he had been drinking milk. There is a blemish on the man's cheek and some freckles scattered over his nose, only densely, so not quite scattered but gathered over his nose, which is to say on his nose which is bulbous at the ends and has medium-sized nostrils. There is the man's speaking voice which has a slight nasal quality, though not unpleasant, a slight under-toning of soprano, perhaps, and some bit, not at all consequential, of shyness or reticence in his offer to "fetch the cap." There is a kind of old world courtliness about the man which is evident not only in his diction but in his eyes which lower modestly away from my rather blunt gaze into them, blunt because of the wish to assess the man's motivations, whether he is normal or up to something unforeseeable, a glint of which I hope to catch in his eyes which lower and avert. There he is taking a long piece of string from the pocket of his dark trousers and tying the end of the string to the v of a twig he snaps from a very small acacia tree growing in the middle of one of the flower beds. There he is dipping the string with the twig end down into the fountain and now scraping my hat, which has the look of bobbing eggplant along the bottom of the fountain bowl which is frothy with bubbling waters. There is me looking at his eyes again, just for that brief second that they meet mine before looking quickly down to his task with the stick and string, and finding in those eyes nothing noteworthy to report, only that the pupils don't waver in size, which I find only slightly disconcerting, and the eyes themselves hold no expression whatsoever, I may as well be looking into x's. There is now a memory creeping into my mind, just a little hint of something, an image of someone with the same eyes from a horror film choking a woman, first the eyes are what I recall and then the thumbs on the woman's neck which are also very distinctive. There is the man now reaching into the fountain once more and this time coming up with my new hat, which is of course sodden and unwearable, looking more like a dead animal—a rat or a fish—than a once perky, beloved hat. There are the man's thumbs which are similar in shape to the ones of the horror film murderer and there is the man smiling very broadly at me as he holds forth the hat, very proud is his smile and there is a tooth missing, a bicuspid. There is also a tear on the man's plaid shirt right over his heart and triangular so that I can see a section of his nipple, which is very almost shockingly pink, like a woman's. There I am wringing out my hat in the fountain and thanking the man for his trouble, careful now not to make eye contact, but just intent on the wringing motion, which is the motion of my two fists going in opposite directions. There is the man sitting on the edge of the fountain and watching me wring out my hat, making no attempt to leave on his bicycle and also the sky is turning a violet color right over the tops of the mountains and the breeze which was at first slight, then heavy, then slight again, is at this point picking up so that the man's bicycle jiggles precariously on its kickstand and then topples over making a crashing sound which startles me more than I might have predicted. There is the man righting the bicycle and, at the same time, there I am mumbling goodbye to the man and thanks again, feeling a little squeamish now and not grateful enough, therefore feeling also guilty but squeamish nonetheless. There is a creeping feeling across the back of my neck and there is my heart pounding and there is the sky turning navy blue. There are flowers which are now dark clumps in their shallow concrete beds, as are the dark silhouetted shapes of the religious leader and his wife who are so fondly depicted here, along with the joyous dancing-in-a-circle, ring-around-the-rosy children from another century, looking and feeling so peaceful and safe, peaceful because safe, in that order, among the gardens of their youths, which is to say the gardens of all of our youths, so filled as they were with happiness and innocence. There I am walking among all this beauty and kindness and benevolence while behind me there is the unmistakable sound of someone taking measured steps so as neither to pass nor lag, also the sound of a creaky wheel, a kind of rolling along sound with a little glitch in it, and a clinking chain which is very rhythmic and to my mind portentous. There I am walking alone toward the stone staircase which will take me out of the garden into the real world of traffic and darkness, where the dark I see from here over the top of the stairs is solid but nevertheless lit by the various moving and wavering car headlights and the more stationary and reliable streetlights and the occasional flashlight shone into the all but impenetrable night by someone who intends to either light our way or blind us.

THREE SEASIDE
TALES

The Man With the Spotted Dog

I was sitting at an outdoor cafe across from the ocean in Florida when I spotted the man with the spotted dog. I thought it was interesting. Me at a seaside resort and a man with a spotted dog. It reminded me of the famous story where a man meets a lady with a dog, also at a seaside resort, and has a long-term affair with her. A story noted for its pathos and irony, a particular combination of which characterizes the renowned author of the renowned story.

So. There I was in my short shorts, gazing wearily at the spider veins in my legs, waiting for fate to intervene in my life. Thus I was melancholy, thinking of life's great themes—disintegration and death, loss and heartache—when the man with the spotted dog sat at the adjoining table. The dog was small, but muscular and ill-tempered. It strained against its leash and yelped annoyingly. The man shook open his *New York Times* and ignored the dog. He wore navy blue shorts with an orange stripe, a beige baseball cap, and designer sunglasses. His legs were tan. His fingers were ringless. His toenails were manicured.

As I studied what parts of him were available around his newspaper, his dog barked angrily. At me, I suddenly realized. "Quiet!" I was gearing up to say to the dog, when the man folded his newspaper and addressed me. "Are you wearing perfume? The dog hates perfume."

I wasn't wearing perfume. "I never wear perfume," I said.

"Come over here, so you won't have to shout," said the man.

That was how I first came to know the man and his dog. They were from Connecticut. It'd been a long time since I'd been to Connecticut. When I thought of Connecticut, I thought of the woods and pine needle floors and muddy streams with skinny, silver-colored minnows.

"You wouldn't know it anymore," said the man mournfully. "It's all urbanized and squalid."

That night we went on a date and the dog came along. "I just can't leave him at the motel," said the man.

We went to a restaurant several blocks from the ocean where all the personnel wore lederhosen and Tyrolean hats. Our table had an absurd centerpiece which consisted of a rubber mermaid trapped in an oblong of frozen plastic, adorned with snakes and roses.

"That thing is really hideous," I said.

"Well, I wouldn't know. I try not to be critical," said the man. The dog licked my ankles and the tops of my shoes.

I decided to go out with the man for the following reasons: I happened to be in Florida visiting my elderly aunts who were both nearly stone deaf and spent their days and evenings in very small quarters at the Salt & Palm Condominium shouting at each other. I had been sleeping on the foldout sofa in the living room and I felt as though I were always caught in their crossfire. Also, Bessie and Fran were not cooks. For dinner we ate things like hard-boiled eggs and leftover Domino's pizza. I was in the mood for a real dinner. Also, the man was good-looking in a sulky sort of way. He had dark eyebrows that almost connected into one brow over the bridge of his nose. And his teeth were ok, very straight and white, no spaces. Other than those meager physical attributes, it's true he was not charming, even though he was obviously well-educated and liked animals.

Now I was beginning to fear that, really, we had nothing in common and the dinner would be one long, painful drudgery, face to face, chewing and swallowing. The dog was extremely irritating, my ankle was beginning to chafe from the action of its tongue. The Bavarian-attired wait-people were relentlessly cheerful in a bluff, over-hearty, Germanic sort of way, and in a corner of the bar a group of customers had gathered to sing beer-hall songs. I hated everything about this place. The concept of bratwurst nauseated me.

"You're not a fan of the food? You should have said something."

The man, I now noticed, had an almost imperceptible smugness about his mouth, some small pursing of the lips with which he communicated his disapproval. I imagined him as a small child with a mother whose mouth he learned to imitate. I could picture him very clearly picking up his toys, making towers with his little alphabet blocks. Even as a child, very clean. His lips beginning that prissy pursing. The more I imagined the man as a boy—screaming if his food items touched, washing his hands compulsively after riding a bus— the less likely it seemed he would ever own a dog, much less one who slobbered over my instep.

Now sprang to mind a picture of the man growing up in Connecticut near a big city in a white house with black shutters. His father, who had business internationally, was hardly ever at home. His mother, moody and removed, insisted upon certain standards of hygiene. I saw the boy, in impeccable slacks and shirt, standing forlornly on the sidelines while neighborhood kids tossed a football amongst themselves. A cast in one eye, he always appeared to be abstracted, inattentive. For this reason, teachers distrusted him, and one teacher went so far as to yank him brutally out of the cafeteria line and seat him in the cloakroom for twenty minutes. There among the damp smelling coats and galoshes he gazed out of a tiny, grimy window to a tiny, tremulous landscape. It seemed to represent his future: a sky with a moist cloud, a shaggy tree, and a dog with a few spots racing through...

Oh, Chekhov! Where are you now? Because I want to wrap up this story of the man with the spotted dog, which is to say that I wanted the evening to be over. I yearned to settle myself into the lumpy heft of the foldout sofa and listen to Bessie and Fran argue about laundry. But mostly I wanted the man on the other side of the trapped mermaid centerpiece to become kinder and more accessible and funnier—to lean across the table, to take my hand in his. "Darling," he would say with charming insincerity, "I have been waiting for you always and now it is our good fortune to meet at last."

MARY ANN

If you see a colored person sitting on the bench in front of the Salt & Palm Condominium in Boca Raton, Florida, do not think she is a resident. No, she is working for somebody, waiting for her ride. She is probably a visiting nurse come to give someone an enema. Or a maid. At the front desk Jacob buzzes in the visitors and others. Those he doesn't recognize he telephones about. The carpet in the lobby is bright green with a band of paler green running up and down its angles, like a lawn, only more everlasting. There are stripes everywhere on the upholstery and a glass-topped coffee table in the shape of a swimming pool and a multitude of fake plants. Once in a while someone puts a real vase of flowers on the table and this fools everyone who is used to the artificial. It is hard to tell what from what. I am very sleepy.

My employer is called Jim M_____. I'm obliterating the last name in case he recognizes himself in this story I intend to publish and decides to sue. Not that he is the type to sue. These people, as a rule, don't sue. Also, Mr. M_____, who I do not mean to slander, has had a stroke and is very forgetful and disoriented, which is why I am here.

During the day I push him to the poolside in his wheelchair. His yellow sweater is around his shoulders, and on his head is a canvas hat with a plaid band. To me, he is very beautiful—small bones, tiny flat ears, his slacks always with a good crease and nice shoes with white laces. His hair is silver and as thin as a halo and exceptionally well-behaved. As is Jim himself, a perfect gentleman even though he is highly confused and does not always know which end is up. Poor Jim. In private I call him Jim.

"Penny for your thoughts," he said the other day. He stretched his trembly hand toward me which was the signal for handholding. I am sure there are those who see us around the pool and feel—I am trying to imagine what they feel— disgusted.

Mrs. M_____, who I always call Mrs. M_____, is sometimes, I am sure, embarrassed by his behavior. "Give us a little kiss," he said the other day to the daughter of one of the residents. I had to laugh to myself because the daughter, who I will call Louise, took a backwards step and almost fell into the pool. She had dark hair twisted up and kept in place with a wooden spike. "That's a nice thing," I told her about the spike. Then she kissed him and a look crossed her face. I know the feeling. His cheek like a moth, as if you were kissing something fluttering, about to fly apart. One good swat and the pieces of Mr. M_____ would turn to dust. I like my job.

Mrs. M_____ is the opposite. She has a wedge-shaped body—skinny legs, huge torso. When she plunges into the water, she creates an enormous fan-shaped spray on either side of her top-half, like the prow of a ship. She has a very forceful voice and is of course much more practical than Mr. M_____. You'd never catch Mrs. M_____ smiling at a bird or throwing pebbles to a baby. You'd never catch her dribbling a little water on her pant leg just to watch the spot spread out. She does everything very fast—zip zip zip—she swims, she towels, she slaps on the Coppertone, she showers, she eats. She tells me, "Don't you think he needs a sweater today? It's a little chilly." Or "I was thinking he might like a ham sandwich and a pickle and I'll have the same, thank you dear." Mrs. M_____ and I do not have conversations and she never calls me by my name. In both these ways she's like my mother.

My mother who is not a maid and says she would never be a maid for any white people, God strike her dead. "Mama, I'm not a maid. I am a companion. A companion is different from a maid," I explain. "Idiot," she says. "Do you or do you not fix theys lunches?" "I may, on occasion, make a sandwich for two old people who can no longer do for themselves, yes, mother." "Do you or do you not vacuum clean? Do you or do you not wash theys dishes?" My mother has eyes that could snap off the branch of a tree. "Answer me that."

This is what's true: When I go home at night I am still in some part of my brain at the Salt & Palm sitting beside Jim and holding his hand or giving him sips of water from a paper cone or folding his yellow sweater and putting it on a shelf in his closet. I am still there with him in the living room on the gold sofa looking through the drapes with the parrot print at the waterway boats and the shimmery grey waves and the beautiful flower beds and lawns.

I know you are thinking the obvious, but it is not that simple. I do not want their *things*. What I would like is to be able to fall asleep in his California King with the lacy pillow-cases—not for the purpose of luxury, but for the purpose of *understanding*. This is what you have to realize about me since this is the story of me, I am its main character and Mr. M_____ and Mrs. M_____ and all the folks around the pool and crossing and recrossing the green carpeting are subsidiary to me. Which is not the same in real life.

Here is my main point: the Salt & Palm Condominium, situated on a strip of land bordering the Gulf Stream Waterway in Boca Raton, Florida, is a sand-colored building whose insides duplicate the lawn and the hedges surrounding it. There are one, two, and three bedroom units. Each has a balcony that overlooks the waterway and the harbor full of tall, drifting boats. The youngest inhabitants are in their 60's and the oldest are pushing 100. Mostly retirees, though there are one or two well-preserved blond ladies who have jobs in the village. These are the questions which arise: what do the inhabitants of the Salt & Palm think about all day? And also: how is it that they take it all in stride? The boxy hedge and the gardeners who clip them, the poolside geraniums, the unwavering lawn, the waterway with its silver dazzles clucking around the little dock? The white plastic chaises, the grandchildren, the lunchtimes and dinnertimes, the clear pool always without bugs and twigs, the chrome railings gleaming like celestial bodies? And those other bodies with pedicures and hairdos and the lazy, ringed, freckled fingers reaching for the Bain de Soleil? And the slick, orange, hairless legs? Because I don't understand what these bodies contain other than themselves. As a student of creative writing, I am compelled to explore what baffles me. Oh, I am so tired sometimes I wish I were dead.

To be truthful, I'm a little in love with Jim. Of all the bodies here, his is the most delicate and lovely. His skin is the color of glass. If you stand behind him at a certain time of day, you can see through the tip of his ear. Lord Jim, I call him, after one of those big schooners that comes into the waterway. When Louise heard me say it, she said, "Oh, Conrad," showing off. She and I have gotten friendly. "These people," she hisses—Louise hisses—"are total bigots. I just hope you realize that." She means well but she is not a writer. She doesn't have the curiosity to put up with things. I try to explain about Mrs. M_____'s nightgown, a full-length night-gown, pure white with pale blue satin bows on the lace straps and little tucks above a cluster of snowy pleats. I tell her that for me the nightgown—much too small for Mrs. M_____ now—is a symbol. "You're a romantic," Louise says.

At home my mother makes an apple pie. She is standing in her bra, rolling out the crust. She swears a blue streak. She hates making pies. Now here is a person whose insides are full of crevices and whorls. Also, she is divorced. She's always reminded me of that tragic fact. "I am a divorced woman, Mary Ann, and in this world a single woman better know where she's at or there'll be hell to pay to the piper." She is still mad at me for working at the Salt & Palm, even though it brings a good income. "Shit and damn," she says as she flops the crust into a glass dish. The kitchen light is grimy and dim due to the one bulb that's burned out in the over-head fixture. When she tried to repair it the other day, a little explosion followed by a shower of sparks occurred, so she said she better let sleeping dogs lie. I wanted to point out that there was nothing "sleeping" about a near electrocution, but these days she is so prickly with me I did not dare. As a creative writing exercise, I take note of things as if for the first time: the row of metal canisters with dents on each of the lids, the lettering all faded on the SUGAR, a pile of laundry on a chair, shoes under the table since last week. Through our window with the dusty yellow valance, a depressing view of Mr. Oliphant's old rusted Ford Falcon and our own clothesline with a green towel slapping in the wind. All this reminds me of the Salt & Palm and its calmness and beauty. I hear some kids screaming on their bicycles and I cannot help but make a comparison.

My mother scratches under the strap of her bra. "Fuck and hell," she says, "I got to lose some of this poundage or my underwear won't fit me." In figure she is not unlike Mrs. M_____, though I have never seen, nor do I wish to see, Mrs. M_____ in a bra.

Once the pie's in the oven Mama looks me over. Her eyes are hot and instinctively I flinch as if she would hit me, though she's never hit me. "What you looking at?" she says. "I know what you're thinking, don't think I don't." She looks around the room and I see a small sadness crease her face before she marches out.

This is when I recall with shame what I did today when Mrs. M_____ had gone shopping and Mr. M_____ was taking his P.M. nap. I went to the closet and removed the nightgown from its pink hanger. At first I only held it up to the window. It was so beautiful, the light poured into it and dazzled on the snowy pleats, the little tucks underneath the bodice. Then, I could not help it, I tried it on. In the full-length I looked a way in which I'd never seen myself: as if the light had filled my body as well as the nightgown. You may think this is a vague metaphor but it is the truth. I had become the light and I had also become the nightgown. I myself: snowy, white, soft. I wish I could describe the feeling. At first I wanted to cry and then I became dizzy. Luckily, I managed to take it off and neatly replace it on its pink hanger before Mrs. M_____ returned. Then I walked over to Jim who was still napping, his head to one side on the pillow and drool coming out of the side of his lip. It crossed my mind I could kill him so easily. Just pick up the pillow and stuff it in his face. It wouldn't take hardly any strength.

I am looking out the window at the clothesline and it's getting darker outside so that the green towel that flapped a few moments ago is a flapping silhouette that reminds me of a bat. I've always been good at description. Mr. Oliphant's old, rusty car is a medium-sized whale against the grey sky and the one or two smudged stars which are trying to shine on our roof are like bottle caps at the bottom of a puddle. Of course, I do not really want a nightgown such as the one I tried on this afternoon. What I want is the *feeling* of the nightgown. But, as I've already mentioned, it is hard to write down exactly what the feeling is. When I figure it out, I will insert it into this story which I believe is drawing to a close.

THE PHANTOM SHIP

After a while a white ship pulls into the waterway. Looming over everything—the palm trees and the swimming pool and the buildings that comprise the Salt & Palm Condominium—it reminds us of a whale. It intrudes into our peaceful scenario where we are sunbathing and reading our novel, filling us with awe and dread. It is so big, for one thing, and so close. If it were a different kind of vehicle it would mow us down in our bikinis on our plastic chaises. It would flatten the hibiscus shrub and the sea grass and the little spider who makes her home in the deep nooks of the gardenia.

The sun moves behind a cloud and now we can look up, up, as high as the top deck of the ship, as high as the row of portholes adjoining the top deck of the ship. No one. No one languishing over the railings, no one pining at the windows. This is, we decide, The Phantom Ship, driven by the waterway ghosts who are laughing invisibly on the top deck, throwing their heads back and sipping cocktails out of blue stemmed glasses. They are still in their evening clothes. The one called Marie wears her hair in a chignon; she is leaning her black-stockinged leg against Charles, who appears lost in thought. "He is dreaming with his eyes open," says Priscilla, his mother. Other couples drift and float: a tall blond woman dances with a tall blond man. A burly fellow with a moustache storms by shaking his fist at Fred, the bellhop, who shivers in his red coat.

"Of what does Charles dream?" asks Marie, who is sad to be ignored by her handsome fiancé.

"He dreams always of a ship," says his mother, who knows him best.

"Always the same dream?"

The mother settles her enormous weight onto a deck chair which creaks as she sits. "Yes. Always the same. I will tell it to you.

"A young man in search of his fortune sets sail on a lavish ocean liner. There he finds himself in the private stateroom of a beautiful woman and her companion, an older man with intensely blue eyes. There is a marble fireplace, a mantel adorned with yellow roses, wallpaper with a pattern of dense, green vines, a velvet chair, a silver tea service on a hammered brass table, an ottoman covered with silk monkeys, a Persian rug featuring stick figures scurrying up a ladder, a leather-bound volume of Heraclitus, and a cat. The cat sits on the woman's lap purring softly as she strokes it with a gloved hand. Her companion paces in front of the fire which shoots up its blazing pinnacles behind him, crackling and hissing, as if parodying the man's restless mood. The window is a dark square framed by a shimmering drapery. 'Oh wonder of wonders,' the woman is saying, 'I wonder where I left my handkerchief.'

"The woman and the man proceed to talk to each other in low voices, too muted for the dreamer to hear. It is as if he were invisible to them as they are inaudible to him, as if a thick transparent substance separates the dreamer from the dream. It occurs to him to test this theory by snatching the cat from the woman's lap. As he predicted, he is unable to do so—his hand encounters something implacable which holds it in check. Thus he sprawls on the rug and contents himself with studying the woman—her lovely brown eyes, the paleness of her skin, her hair which is auburn and curled. She is familiar to him, the way her hands stroke the cat, even the rings on her fingers—he feels as if he's seen them before when he was much younger, perhaps in a dream.

"He is startled by a movement in the dense vines of the wallpaper behind her head. A little man, no more than two inches long, is crawling along, hoisting his tiny body up and over the tangle of spindly vines, balancing himself now and then on the wide palettes of the leaves. He is on his way to rescue his wife who is trapped under the spider who has made her home in the deep nooks of the gardenia. On and on he climbs, the faint cries of his wife peppering the distance between them. Just then there is a terrible noise which brings the dreamer back to himself. The woman stroking the cat has just shot the man pacing in front of the fireplace. She sits with a puzzled look on her face, staring at the tip of the smoking revolver. 'What should I do now?' she asks the dreamer. She looks so helpless, vulnerable. He wracks his mind for some comforting words to say to her, but just then he wakes up."

"Always at the same point?" asks Marie, fingering the moire of Charles' cuff.

"Always," says Priscilla, his mother, smiling fondly at her son who at this moment is snapping into an elated consciousness. "Marie!" he says, kissing his fiancée passionately.

Overhead, a jet soars, and the sides of the enormous phantom ship tremble and dip.

And the little wife, will she be saved? Will her valiant husband continue to swing and climb toward her? From here her cries pepper the distance like the cries of a cricket or the chattering of ice cubes. Our fingers mark the page in our novel which begins: "He spoke no more, but after a pause softly groped his way out of the room..." So too, The Phantom Ship gropes softly down the waterway. Where to? Who knows?

SECRET
ENCOUNTERS

WRECKAGE

Systematically and with the loftiest intentions, M is destroying his house. He let the grass go at the same time he decided to rebuild his deck. Since he never got any further than taking apart the planks of the deck, they lie now on the brown tough grass, what had been green, fairly resilient grass. When the hot water in the upstairs shower ceased to function, he stopped using the upstairs bathroom, then months later decided on a course of action which was this: saw a jagged hole in the plasterboard and replace a network of pipes. But it's an old house with nonstandard pipes and he has inadequate tools. Now he has no hot water in his house and he uses the neighbor's house for a shower.

SLEEP

E has checked herself into a sleep clinic. She is brought to a room with a wedding ring quilt (she recognizes the pattern) and hooked up to many, many electrodes by a technician called Kathleen. Kathleen tells E she has hidden a microscope somewhere on her person (where? E doesn't ask, but it plagues her throughout the night, just one of many things which will interfere with her sleep) and that if she wants anything, anything at all, she should call *Kathleen! Kathleen!* and Kathleen will rush to the bedside.

FACE

K is having her face refurbished: eyelids, upper and lower, and a chemical peel which is supposed to leave her wrinkle-free. She is very nervous pre-surgery, then relaxed post-surgery (it didn't hurt), then very nervous again when she sees her face in the mirror, which, day by day, is getting more grotesque and unfamiliar. Swelling, bruising, skin as livid as the purple tee shirt which she wears every day for the first week of her recovery (why bother?) and finally terrible under-the-skin cystic zits the likes of which she never encountered in her teens. What was wrong with my old face? she wonders now, knowing also that regret is a hopeless and doomed path, the path to suicidal depression or murder.

WRECKAGE

M has decided to smash another hole into the plaster above the sink. Somewhere there must be a pipe that he can remove easily and replace and then perhaps the toilet, which stopped flushing, will work. Outside, the sprinkler system is on day and night but the grass is irredeemable, according to his neighbor whom he ignores except at shower time. The water from the sprinklers glides off the former lawn like water off a duck's back, as the saying goes, and down the concrete steps where it puddles up in this same neighbor's carport. Despite all these mishaps, M fancies himself as one who is handy around the house. Didn't he purchase a dining room table, barely scratched, for $250? And how about that leather chair, the envy of all who come to visit? Still, the house is slowly dissolving, even as he works to remedy the dissolution—the grass, the pipes, the various carpentry disasters like the time he decided to replace the kitchen cabinets, tore them out, then discovered the expense of new ones.

SLEEP

E is having trouble sleeping. In the next room over, a Tongan man is snoring ridiculously, a series of beefy glottal sounds that shake the walls not rhythmically but erratically, causing E to shudder with each liquidy eruption. Lying in the darkened room of the clinic, hooked up to numerous electrodes, wrapped in the thin wedding ring quilt, E imagines the Tongan man's wife angrily dispatching him to the clinic with the admonition not to return until cured. How would you spell that sound? Tchrrrrrah, fluuuuugh, KLLLLPPP? But E really, really has to go to the bathroom. Kathleen! she calls. KATHLEEN! she calls again, on and on. She begins what will be a two-hour search for the hidden microphone.

FACE

K's face now fills her with dread. She imagines the poor homeless persons who could have been helped by the 10 thou she gave over to the plastic surgeon and this fills her with dread too, as if she'd deliberately created terrible karma for herself. Her Saturn return occurs in two weeks and now she knows what the rest of her life will be like—punishment for wrong decisions, ugliness, old age, death. To distract herself from the debacle of her face, she turns to a network special on the paranormal. The master of ceremonies is a tall, eager, Regis Philbin type of host, who has great enthusiasm for his topic and guests, all of whom are paranormal experts. The first guest is a man who tracks the aura of someone's car—a white Lincoln—to the parking lot of the studio; the second is a rather strident hypnotist who bullies a pale audience member into a deep sleep, then has her relive a very short (two minute) part of a past life.

WRECKAGE

M is exhausted. All this work for so little reward. He sits heavily on his leather chair and glances at a newspaper, gets up, paces to the kitchen, opens a cupboard which houses a jug of white wine vinegar, box of toothpicks, jar of oregano, and unopened package of paper napkins. He throws out the toothpicks, thinks the better of it, retrieves them, selects one and digs into a crevice between two molars until he draws blood. When the phone rings he checks his caller ID, decides not to answer, picks up the paper, sits heavily on the leather chair.

SLEEP

Kathleen accompanies E to the ladies room. She must make quite a picture walking along with all the electrodes dangling from the places to which they've been affixed. On the way back she glimpses the Tongan man through his half-opened door, sleeping like a baby.

FACE

The highlight of the paranormal special involves a trance channeler who will channel the spirits of Marilyn Monroe and Andy Kaufman. Present at the scene of the channeling are Marilyn's first husband, a dissolute-looking man with a white beard, and Andy Kaufman's former girlfriend and former producer, who are convinced that Andy spoke to them through the medium. He's the real thing, says the producer, wiping tears. He said things that only the most intimate of Andy's acquaintances could have known.

WRECKAGE

After a short respite in which he drank a glass of red wine, M is busy with a screwdriver and a doorknob. The doorknob never worked properly and now he'll fix it. He needs a break from the plumbing activities which only frustrate him. It feels that the more he tinkers with pipes and fittings and water shut-off-valves, the less he knows. He is confident that the solution will occur to him just as in his job as computer programmer he often comes upon a solution in his mind's eye, floating by innocently, unaware of being sought after. But for now he will busy himself with screwdriver and doorknob and, because when things can go wrong they do go wrong, he happens to have the wrong kind of screwdriver, a screwdriver whose head does not quite grip the groove in the screw it must turn.

SLEEP

E is trying to sleep. A skinny rim of light can be seen at the bottom of the window shade, but otherwise the room is a model of sensory deprivation. She has an electrode in her nose and several on her legs but most have been glued into her hair where they monitor E's brain activity, possibly even her irritation at this minute. She still doesn't know where the microphone has been hidden. The Tongan man continues to snore, of course, so in this sense the room is not a model of sensory deprivation. She fingers the capsule in her nostril and wonders if this is the microphone. Hello! Hello! she imagines shouting. Calling all cars!

FACE

Uri Gellar and his spoons are, of course, the grand finale. On her way to the kitchen to retrieve a few spoons for the home audience experiment, K catches a glimpse of her new ten-thousand-dollar face in the mirror—horrible! Her eyes are red slits in a gargantuan face. She looks like a character from Star Trek. She looks nothing like herself and now she yearns for herself, the self she so breezily surrendered to the surgeon's knife. The little wrinkled dear self with pouches under the eyes and slack cheeks. She selects a tarnished silver-plated spoon to surrender to Uri Gellar's ministrations. While she's at it, she grabs a broken wristwatch from the bureau and her car keys.

WRECKAGE

Nothing is easy in this life. Screwdrivers never fit the right screw heads, hammers hide in garages or cellars under paper bags or heaps of laundry, stove burners jam inexplicably, the deck planks which you intended to refinish have warped on the lawn which has turned the color of granite. M's downstairs toilet is now on the fritz. He thinks this may be due to the woman who visited last Thursday. He met this woman via an Internet dating service and after a three week correspondence, during which he shared his fantasies about their marriage and parenthood, she arrived in his city. She came to his home, knocked on the door, and said *Surprise!* In the course of the evening she used his toilet, after which it broke. It was sad; he didn't think he could love her.

SLEEP

Amazingly, at the sleep clinic, amid the racket of the Tongan man's snores and despite the electrodes which feel like spiders crawling on her skin and in her hair, E has a dream. She dreams she is married to a nice but boring man and that they have two beautiful daughters, Crissa and Cressa. The daughters take violin lessons and diving lessons and rollerblade lessons and attend an experimental school where all grade levels mingle in one large room and the method of education involves going from area to area with teachers' aides. E sometimes volunteers at the school, which is run by two lesbians, and teaches the children papier-mâché. At night she wracks her brain over what to serve the boring husband for dinner since, in addition to being boring, he is demanding about meals. He prefers meals like pork chops and meatloaf, while she is inclined toward snacks: California rolls that she meticulously handcrafts (her speciality), snippets of carrot and cucumber on hard-boiled eggs, cheese and toast, yogurt shakes. So she wracks her brain in search of healthful compromises. The husband likes a routine: Mondays, pork chops; Tuesdays, steak; Wednesdays, lasagne; and so on. But E confuses the weekday meals. He is victimized, he claims, by her unpleasant surprises. At school she works on large papier-mâché animals—elephants, tyrannosaurus, and alligators, all with movable mouths and as big as pieces of playground equipment. At night she has trouble sleeping, tossing and turning, then finally rising and going to the window, looking out over

41

the mountains which surround this city and at the moon's dead weight in the sky. At around 7 in the morning she falls asleep on the living room couch. Then her day starts all over again.

FACE

Uri Gellar collects a group of children from the audience. They surround him, these children, in an unruly circle. He bids them to crowd in closely as he picks up a spoon. Concentrate, he says to the children, and then Uri begins to rub very softly the stem of the spoon; very, very softly he rubs, and he closes his eyes, and around him the children's eyes are closed, and Uri Gellar is saying *bend,* and the children are repeating the word *bend*. Then a look of distress passes over Uri's face; he opens his eyes. This doesn't always work, he says. He looks straight into the camera: I CAN'T ALWAYS GET IT TO WORK SO YOU MUST HELP ME. Not only the children, but studio audience members and home audience members. Pick up your own spoons and say *bend* and visualize the spoon bending, melting. K does this. She holds her spoon in her left hand and with her right hand she rubs the stem: *bend*, she says. She is studying the faces of the children gathered around Uri Gellar: she is not surprised to see that some appear to be cynical and embarrassed. One tall boy in particular keeps flicking his eyes open and barely enunciates the word *bend*, as if humiliated to have been selected for this display. When Uri's spoon not only bends but snaps in two, there is a tremendous audience applause. The children look happy and successful and Uri warmly hugs the ones nearest to him. The TV camera pans the audience and many are holding up their own bent and twisted spoons for camera display. K's spoon hasn't bent at all. Nor, in the following segment, does her broken watch begin to tick. After the show, she takes her spoon to the kitchen and digs it into a pint of Ben and Jerry's cookie dough ice cream.

WRECKAGE

When the woman arrived at M's door wearing a fur coat, black and white harem pants, thick mittens that might have belonged to a child, and a fringed orange scarf, M thought at first she was a Jehovah Witness and positioned his body in such a way as to block her view of the hall, which was heaped with tools and torn-up plasterboard upon a grey tarp. *Surprise!* said the woman. It was then that M took note of her long nose and a certain toothiness of smile whose implication was intimate and familiar. He considered she might be a relative, but then a light bulb went off and he realized it must be Sharon, his email entanglement. She stood there, a sturdy little bundle, looking more like a Russian peasant than a volleyball coach (which is what she was). Right away he knew it was impossible; no, no, he could never love her. Why did she have to come right when he was in the middle of fixing things up? But she did come and she sat on the leather chair and admired its comfort and looked around the room as if assessing the value of its contents. What happened there? she asked in reference to a few lengths of pried up floorboards. Then she asked to use the toilet.

SLEEP

When she awakes from this dream, E realizes that she has dreamed her life, that the boring husband and two beautiful daughters (though their names were not Crissa and Cressa) were waiting for her to return from the sleep clinic. It must be morning, she imagines, but she has no idea. Her watch is in the pocket of her jacket which is on a chair just out of reach of the bed. She tries to reach it anyway. She leans over the side of the bed, careful of the electrode connection to the monitor and tries to grab an edge of the jacket. It's only inches away, but it might as well be in Chicago.

FACE

K used to have dreams of a perfect face: no bags, no wrinkles, skin as silky as a model's, eyes wide, green and fringed with a double row of lashes, sultry lips whose corners turned up charmingly instead of down as if, she told herself pre-surgery, she were caught in the throes of revulsion. She is confined to her house still, her face a lumpy mass of mottled flesh, her eyes surrounded by black stitches like Frankenstein's monster. Though her vision is still bleary, she decides the only way to get through this terrible time is to absorb herself in a book. Thus, she reads a story about a man who is in love with his neighbor but doesn't know it. This man depends on this neighbor for gardening tips, dinners, showers (his own is broken) and even, though he would never acknowledge it, home repair advice. She also offers him companionship, walks in the hills, movie dates, TV watching company, and so forth. The only problem is that he doesn't realize the extent to which he has come to take her for granted in his life. So on he goes, blithely ignoring her worth, making dates with women he meets under dubious circumstances, like on the Web. Then there comes a day when the neighbor meets a very young and attractive man who falls passionately in love with her. It is only then that the man realizes what he has lost and, to punish himself for his stupid blindness, sets about destroying his house.

WRECKAGE

After she broke his toilet (did she flush a tampon or what?), Sharon discussed with M her sexual proclivities. Without her fur coat and her scarf she looked not nearly so sturdy and Russian, though around her shoulders and forearms, she exhibited distinct muscle clumps, à la the volleyball coach that she is. She told him she's into S & M. Really? he said. Unbidden to his mind's eye came a barn's interior with a horse whip draped over a rusty hook. I'm a submissive, she said. I enjoy being tied up and tormented very, very playfully. I'm not into any real pain. Excited and curious, M escorted her to his bedroom, where he eventually tied her naked body to the closet door (which was hanging by only one hinge) and prodded her orifices with a screwdriver and an old pipe. Very, very nice, she screamed, oh, how very nice you are to me! Oh, how good you are! Sharon kept screaming, until M could no longer stand the shame and he went into his bathroom to take a shower, then remembered he couldn't on account of the hot water.

SLEEP

So at 6 AM on the button, Kathleen wakes E. Rise and shine! Time to go home! she says. E has just gotten off to sleep, of course, of course. But when Kathleen removes the electrodes, E feels paradoxically burdened, as if her life has been temporarily out of her hands and now is rushing back to settle in awkwardly. Thus encumbered, she makes her way to the front desk where she is required to fill out a form. How long do you think you slept? is one of the questions. *About fifteen minutes,* E writes, then thinks the better of it, crosses it out, and writes *one hour.* As she hands the form to Kathleen who, at this time of the morning is not nearly so sprightly, she can't help but catch a glimpse of the Tongan man on the monitor, still sleeping soundly. Why is the Tongan man allowed to sleep in? she wonders as she leaves the building, and the more she thinks about it the more it strikes her as inexplicable, and thus unfair, and thus characteristic of her luck. Outside a lovely day is in progress, the tall, green treetops rustle and dip over the streets, causing long, fluttery shadows, but it is at least an hour before her children and her boring husband wake up, so she drives to a café she knows will be open this early. Aside from a woman wearing dark glasses and a floppy green hat who sits at a corner table eating a scone, there is no one in the place.

FACE

It is hard to imagine a future when one is hamstrung by the present. This is the way K had imagined her old face, as that which hamstrung her future. Now, almost painlessly, she has a new face, eyes that are wide and luminous, skin that is taut though still pinkish and swollen. She is disturbed by what one might call an implacable look, her eyes somewhat devoid of expression, a hardness of cheekbone and jaw, but this, she supposes, is a small price to pay for looking fifteen years younger. She ventures out this morning, very early, wearing her wide-brimmed hat and sunglasses and walks to a neighborhood café. She is a little sad as she reminisces about what had prompted her to spend ten-thousand dollars refurbishing her face to begin with: she had been thrown over by her young lover. You are too old, he told her.

46

WRECKAGE

M is taking a shower at the neighbor's. He let himself in the back door, then crept up her staircase to the upstairs shower. As he sudses himself with a green soap that smells like ham, he imagines the neighbor stumbling half-asleep and naked into the bathroom, and going to the toilet, before she realizes that he is there, a man in her bathroom, taking a shower. He has an urge to sing *Oklahoma*. Probably because *Oklahoma* is a cheery, unromantic song, patriotic in its enthusiasms and very resoundingly loud, loud enough to wake a woman sleeping with her head under her pillow dreaming about spiders. He had left Sharon, his email companion, in his bedroom that evening of a week ago. She'd had to undo the flimsy knots he'd bound her with and she'd eventually left, her eyes shining with either disappointment or hope, he wasn't sure which. He was not unhappy to see her go. During the course of the evening, she'd made several snide remarks about the condition of his home, which did not endear her to him at all.

SLEEP

After two cups of espresso, sleep is the furthest thing from E's mind. She feels wound up and jittery like one of those plastic toys—the clacking teeth or the jumping penis. She has an urge to speak to the woman in the dark glasses and the floppy green hat, if only to utter the sentence she has a compulsion to say, which is this: *working undercover?* An unremarkable sentence, not even a little clever, but she has an almost frantic urge to say it with an amused smile just to see what the woman's reaction will be. Very possibly, the woman will get up and leave, coldly and mysteriously leave, not bothering with a response. But there is a slight chance, isn't there, that she will remove her dark glasses and hat and begin to talk about her life, about the young lover who's pronounced her too old to love, about her surgery which she feared would deform her forever, about her vanity which is endless, endless?

FACE

Whereas the woman across the room drinking espresso has a beautiful face. A strong young face with big, sloped eyebrows, wide lips in a wide mouth. K has been making meticulous studies of women's faces and in this woman's face the brow imparts structure: large, bony, and curved back to the hairline, everything in the face seems to proceed from it; even the lips take on, in reverse, the eloquent arc of the brow and seem to harmonize it. Beauty, in this case, is proportion.

WRECKAGE

Whereas M believes that beauty will be uncovered only after a grueling struggle: tearing at the roof tiles or digging up a section of the garden. And the neighbor, when she makes her entrance, not naked but robed, almost beautiful therefore, is not surprised at his presence in the shower but delighted, laughing, running water and brushing her teeth. We're like an old married couple, she says, which strikes fear in his heart as she knew it would.

SLEEP

And E is not thinking of beauty but of change. If only her life would change, her boring husband go away somewhere and she tries to imagine a life that is not this present life, the life of a woman who owns a motorcycle, for example, and travels across the country riding it, her worldly possessions stuffed in saddle bags. How would it feel to be in the skin of that woman, leaning into the long bends of the freeway, her helmet making a rattling sound near her jaw? And do we always wish for the other life, the life we don't have? She studies the woman in the dark glasses who is apparently studying her as well.

FACE

But it's useless to think these things—to think one could change places with another, thinks K. Because if nothing else we have different faces, hers an edifice of power, like the Empire State Building and mine a sand castle, drippy and vanishing. K rises from her seat and walks to the register and as she passes the gorgeous but melancholy woman, she smiles shyly. Looking down and away, she almost speaks—

WRECKAGE

And M, whose life is bound to change if he prods it along, is beginning another project: refashioning the dining room table. He will sand the scratches off the surface, then stain and seal. The legs are a bit too narrow for the design of the table, he decides, and so those will go too. In fact, those go first. He rips the chainsaw cord and starts in and he is thinking of nothing as he begins, only of the noise of the chainsaw, satisfying and deafening, and the thrill of this beginning, this new beginning, which is not a beginning at all, but an ending, or vice versa.

SAW

1

The premise is this: *What happens when a beautiful woman gets maimed by a chainsaw?*

A woman, call her Fran, is in her backyard one day discussing with a professional by the name of Wade the pruning of branches from her tamarisk tree. The tree is hanging over her swimming pool and keeps clogging up the drains. For at least an hour each day and more after a monsoon, the woman has to get in the pool and stuff her hand into each drain and pull out big plugs of tamarisk needles. It goes without saying that she also must empty the white plastic basket and then over by the apricot tree she has to turn off the pump and pull more needles out of the mesh bag. Finally she calls Wade who has his own tree service and is the cheapest of those advertised in the Yellow Pages. Wade comes immediately. He is a small wiry man who looks about 35. He speaks with a slight Texas drawl, a kind of intonation, which right away amuses Fran. He wears mirrored sunglasses with Day-Glo orange rims and he has a big scar on his forearm.

Got runned over by a tank, he tells Fran. Nam, '68. Runned over twice, forward and back. Crushed every bone in the arm. Take ahold of that there, he tells Fran, who feels squeamish about grabbing a stranger's wrist. Go on, he urges. And when she does she hears a crunching sound within the arm itself, not altogether pleasant.

Well, Wade, she says, let's get on with things. Yes'm, says Wade. He has brought with him a ladder, a rope, and a chainsaw, that's all. No sophisticated equipment, no safety halter, no assistant. There is only Wade who has one good arm since the one with the scar has no longer any sensation, he explains. I do it all with the one arm, he says.

Fran sees her own face in Wade's mirrored sunglasses, her face doubled, her beautiful face distorted of course in the reflection. She is feeling skeptical, although her skepticism is not reflected along with her distorted features.

Are you sure? she says. She turns her head so she won't have to see herself or Wade or his arm anymore. She feels responsible for something, she's not sure what, vaguely guilty. A woman with a swimming pool putting a man's life at risk. Like that.

Wade is surveying her garden which is in its last stages of completion. Her husband has been digging holes for trees. This last hole, the one in the approximate center of a grove of Texas ranger, will be filled with a sweet acacia; then wild flowers along the outskirts, maybe a queen's palm once the tamarisk is trimmed, an ocotillo in the xeriscape.

I see you're planting a tree, says Wade. I love a good tree. I love trees too, says Fran, Who doesn't? Oh, you'd surprise yourself, says Wade. Folks on Sunrise want a whole

Eucalyptus sawed up for a sauna. Course we call those Eucs widow-makers, on account of their tendency to drop branches on folks. Over there, he points to the new hole, now over there I'd put a California pepper. We're putting in a sweet acacia, says Fran, actually. Nope, says Wade, California pepper.

This is when Fran goes into the house. From the window she watches Wade hoist himself, one-armed, from the ladder into the tree, dragging his rope, the chainsaw precariously fitted over his shoulder in a kind of makeshift sling. Then he scoots up the rough bark of the tamarisk, grabbing with the good arm onto whatever branches are available, working his feet and legs where he can, into the V's of the tree and over the tops of some of the larger branches, the ones Fran wants trimmed way back.

At the top, he grins and waves toward her in the house which is when she knows he's been watching and she wonders then how it is he can see her through the window which she always imagined to be opaque in daylight, impenetrable. For a brief moment they gaze at one another, she the beautiful woman in her living room window, framed by the window in her beauty, glowing in a way, and Wade on the limb he will saw off, looking somehow inappropriately joyous, she thinks, as he waves the chainsaw at her and smiles broadly.

It is she who breaks the spell, turning from the window and going into her bedroom where she looks in the mirror, seeing now her face undistorted, flawless, the smooth line of her jaw, her slender neck, her high cheekbones glazed softly by light, her wide-set eyes with their dark lashes. Then, because of guilt, because of a certain nagging remorse, feeling too bourgeois and snobbish and possibly too beautiful and blessed in her life with swimming pool and trees to either plant or fell as she wishes, she goes outside and stands beneath the tree, as if to offer some kind of moral support to Wade with his disability, to participate if only marginally in the tree work which, when she thinks of it, is only the result of her own sloth, her disinclination to spend time unplugging drains.

Hey, Wade calls down, nice to see you, how's the weather down there? He's very high. Fran feels a bit of vertigo looking up at him from this angle. Be careful, she says, and it sounds foolish her telling him to be careful, foolish and improper, as if they had a relationship beyond the professional one.

Here, he says, throwing down his sunglasses, try these on for size. You're squinting. The sunglasses land on the cool deck, remarkably intact. Nothing can bust those suckers, calls Wade cheerfully. Try 'em on, they're just your type of a thing. And then, because how can she not, but feeling incredibly self-conscious nonetheless, and even a bit manipulated, truth be told, this tree person making her feel his arm and now wear his sunglasses, something she is not at all inclined to do under any circumstances because she doesn't like them, they are not her type thing at all, she nevertheless puts them on and keeping her expression serious, sober, she asks him when he will begin to saw the limb.

Ready or not, he says and he pulls the chainsaw cord, amazingly, stuffing the saw under the bad arm and pulling the chain with the hand of the good arm until it roars into activity and then he begins to saw, and flakes of tree bark scatter in the pool and tamarisk needles and she thinks ok, only once more will I have to deal with these damn drains, and then the whole branch starts to creak and Wade says, Gangway, Fran, and she jumps to one side just as the branch comes gliding through the air, as if in slow motion, and lands dully in the pool.

Then in no time, like a monkey or a squirrel, Wade is down the tree and beside her and she hands him his sunglasses, relieved that the operation is over. Very good, she says, having no better words. Good job. Whoo-ee, says Wade. His eyes are light green and there are deep lines around the corners which make him look older. He takes the sunglasses and smiles at her in a way she feels is perhaps too personal, his eyes or mouth lingering a beat too long, coming a bit too close, something.

So, he says. He's rocking on his heels, still holding the chainsaw. Powerful machine. Yes, she says, I can't imagine using one. Try it, he says and he hands it to her and she thinks, fleetingly, this is ridiculous, this stranger is making me do all kinds of things, and he instructs her to hold on tight with the one arm out and to pull the chain and there she is following his instructions and after three tries the saw starts up and it vibrates in her hands and she experiences for an instant the tremendous power of that machine like a weapon, something that could do damage, yes, that was it, the power of it to damage and at the same time to save; it vibrates in her hand and she feels the muscles of her arm contract with the strength needed to hold it steady and this is when she absentmindedly puts out her other hand and, with a terrible groan, almost like the noise of an animal, the chain saw slashes through it.

2

Let's restate the premise: *What happens when a beautiful woman gets her hand entangled in a chainsaw?*

Imagine this woman with her bandaged hand; imagine her life. She has a husband called Raymond and Raymond is most sympathetic. At night he rubs her back, he brings her cups of tea in her favorite Limoges cup and he feeds her little spoonfuls of sherbert when she loses either the will or strength to feed herself. He adores her and the fact that her hand will now be maimed and unsightly seems almost to increase his adoration. He kisses her forehead and dabs the sherbert from the corners of her mouth. He touches her breasts beneath her white cotton nightgown. Her breasts have always excited him, but now they excite him more than ever.

For her part, she watches the top of his head as he bends to unbutton her gown, to take her nipples in his mouth. She gazes in distaste at his pink scalp, where his hair is beginning to thin, at the soft yellowish flakes of dandruff. She is beginning to despise him.

During the day, she tries to do what she'd always done, but this of course is impossible. Gardening has always brought her pleasure and she can no longer garden. At first she tries to pick at the soil with her one hand and a little spade, but it is tiring work and the earth this time of year is too hard to yield to such meek scrabblings. She tries to read, but the book slides from her lap and she loses her place and besides, everything makes her tired these days, even the book which is about canoeing down an African river full of crocodiles and cannibalistic natives. She lets the book slide from her lap, the pages flutter closed, and she eases herself from the chair with difficulty, because she is incredibly tired and also because her body is heavy with the pain emanating from the bandaged hand, a pain which extends beyond the bandage itself and even beyond her body, it seems to her, permeating the walls of the rooms she passes through like a terrible grief-stricken ghost.

Finally, because how could she not, she seeks out her reflection in the mirror and her reflection fills her with horror because it is so much as she'd remembered it. Her beautiful face—the line of her jaw, her lashes, even her expression, her look of beautiful emptiness—has not changed a whit and this is horrifying to her, as if life's vicissitudes have no impact whatsoever on a person. She picks up her husband's razor blade and holds it briefly to her neck.

It is around this time—around the time she is holding the razor blade to her neck—that the doorbell rings. It turns out to be Wade, the tree surgeon. He wonders how she's doing. He brings her a small plant. California pepper, he informs her with a large smile. But this one's a sapling, of course, truth be told, smaller than a sapling, a seedling, you could say. He continues to smile and she notices he is missing teeth toward the back of his mouth. Otherwise his smile pleases her.

She puts the plant on the dining room table and admires it in her way, which is to say she gazes at it steadfastly and with no expression on her face save for a small movement at the corner of her mouth.

How're you doing otherwise? asks Wade. He has a hat crumpled in his hand, she notices, in both hands, he is kneading it, a baseball cap, she thinks. Otherwise? she says. This Wade is a vacuous man, stupid even, she thinks. His sunglasses, the same orange-rimmed ones he'd forced her to try on that day, stick out of his tee shirt pocket. Then he brings her this small tree, this ridiculously emblematic tree.

How's the hand? he coughs, looks at his feet. So obvious, she thinks. His guilt, his shame. Is he afraid I will sue his company? She laughs a little. It wasn't your fault, she says. I have a free will.

At the same time, except for the bandage around her hand, the bandage which is a little soiled at this point, a little grey at the edges, except for that, the woman is still a knockout. Her blond hair is more disheveled than before, true, and her eyes aren't as clear, their blueness blurred, as if she regards him through layers of chiffon veils. He would say he sees confusion there or loss of hope. But perhaps her eyes had always been devoid of hope. He touches her cheek.

Now you are wondering what happens between Wade and this woman. Here is a woman, you are thinking, who maimed her hand in a chainsaw belonging to man who is now touching her cheek. As a result, she is now in the throes of a deep depression. Even the man can see it in her eyes—depression, loss of hope, loss of will. He touches her cheek and is surprised when her body gives a shudder.

Does he go further than this? Does he pursue his advantage, touching her shoulders, then her breasts, then kissing her on the mouth, forcing his tongue between her lips, which surrender passively to him, open softly to him?

When the husband returns that night he is surprised by her resistance. No, she whispers to him late at night when he slides himself against her. No, she says, tightening her body, moving to the edge of the bed. No.

3

The premise remains, with this one small modification: What happens when a beautiful woman is injured but the damage is not visible to anyone, that is to say, that although she wears a small bandage, it has the look of a minor accident, perhaps a burn from the stove, from cooking a scallopine, for example.

It looks at any rate like something which will eventually restore itself and so no one much notices or proffers sympathy, not even in their hearts.

There is the husband, of course, who has abandoned his habit of waiting on her. These nights he says he works late, who knows what he really does, and when he returns she is often asleep or pretending to be. Then he leaves quickly in the morning, not bothering to linger over breakfast. It is as if he can no longer bear to look at her. Though she has not changed; in a way she is more herself than ever.

Wade, on the other hand, visits with frequency, often bringing small gifts—ribbon candy, a globe, a framed photograph of himself in Viet Nam. She wishes she could incinerate the gifts, that she could watch them go up in flames. She has a cruel desire to bring pain to Wade, to punish him for his stupidity which seems vast to her, almost otherworldly. But something in her, some trace of her former compassion (or is it the memory of Wade high in the tamarisk that first afternoon, waving to her with such happy abandon?), something stops her just short of unkindness.

Would you like some tea? she asks him. And when he nods, solemnly these days, for he has caught her mood and wants mainly to please her, she gives a little smile, the first in weeks. Sugar? she asks. Certainly, Fran, he says.

They have taken to sitting quietly on the patio by the pool whose surface is clear of tamarisk needles and even bugs and dust. It is a clear day. The sweet acacia has grown to enormous proportions, leafy with little fuzzy flowers at the ends of the branches and these give a sweet smell. Nearby the California pepper has shot from sapling to young tree, its branches like limbs, she thinks, adolescent and heartwrenching. She is fond of this tree, the first of Wade's gifts to her, and when he planted it that afternoon so many months ago she watched as if from her deepest soul, the form of him bending to the earth, like an angel.

THE
EMERGENCE
OF MODERNISM

I was born with a birthmark on my chin. Not a strawberry or mole, but a minute hill where an indentation should have been. It was as if a pea had been slipped beneath my dermis and I think it cast a tiny shadow. My father hated the birthmark, the fact that his progeny had been born flawed, the fact that the flaw might have emanated from his DNA. I was taken to a series of doctors. Part of the examination entailed searching my body for similar "events" and once someone thought he found one at the base of my spine. Consultants were called, but no consensus could be reached regarding the "double." It was determined that the birthmark was a rare occurrence with a Latinate name meaning "swollen blood vessel."

In sixth grade, I underwent plastic surgery at New York Hospital. Because twenty-two stitches were tied to my bottom teeth, I was forbidden to speak for three weeks. I drank pureed roast beef and string beans. A pink plastic cast of a material resembling a ballet slipper was affixed to my jaw, which gave me the look of a horse.

Talking was the sin of my childhood. I talked during class prayer, the salute to the flag, too loudly in restaurants, in cafeteria lines, church processions, in and out of the cloak room, and at night to my sister when we were supposed to be sleeping. My sister would beg me to stop and she would eventually tell, but even telling didn't stop me. As soon as our parents left the room, having admonished us angrily, I plowed on, talking and fiddling with the radio next to my bed, deliberately creating static as background to the stories I invented to terrify her. I told her about the smothering man and the woman who had her eye singed by lightning. The last story I stole from our real life great Aunt May who apparently lost her eye in a lightning storm. I say "apparently" because our grandmother always disputed this fact, saying that Aunt May had contaminated her eye with poisonous paint. She wore regular glasses with one lens painted white; she never bothered with a glass eye.

Why would anyone say they'd been struck by lightning when they hadn't? In my mind's eye I see Aunt May on the rocking chair, a can of yellow paint in the vicinity, and here comes a stripe of jagged lightning making its way to her eye, cannily avoiding the rest of her face: hair the texture and color of cotton balls, only less sturdy and monochrome, encircling a small, kind, pink face wearing glasses with one white-painted lens. Behind the lens is an eye socket I never got to see; behind the eye socket is a liar.

Terror occurs when one's insides don't match one's outsides. The condition of modernity, I tell my students. I am discussing crowds, the phenomenon of. Walking among strangers and having secrets. "Interiority." Baudelaire captures a whiff of this in his prose poem "The Eyes of the Poor" which begins, "So you would like to know why I hate you today."

The operation was not a success and I was left with a knotted scar where the serene little hill had been. When my father looked at me he saw only the botched operation, which enraged him. Years later I had another operation; same thing. They had perfected the surgery, but not enough. I was left with more scars, one dime-sized wheel of scars overlapping another. My father stopped looking at me; I stopped looking at my father.

A boyfriend once confided that he'd been "put off" by the chin when we first met, but that now he hardly noticed it. What is it that happened there? people once in a while ask. I was born with a flaw that the best technology couldn't remove. A flaw that grew worse with attention.

I tend to wring drama out of everything and when a series of dark red blotches appeared on my forearms, I thought of stigmata. Occasionally my stigmata would burst and blood would run down my arms. Once, in class, a student rushed to my desk with a Kleenex to sop up the blood that was dripping on the floor. I was too wrapped up in the emergence of modernism to notice.

My Aunt May was not a prominent figure in my life. Really, she was an image more than a relative. The whitewashed eyeglass lens. How inexpertly that had been done, as if with

Wite-Out. I imagined her sitting with her glasses on her lap, dabbing the lens with a brush, though you'd think she'd avoid paint. For a short time in my life, I couldn't take my eyes off her.

How would you define emptiness: Aunt May's eye socket or the space within the socket? Gertrude Stein's first lover was called May and once, pissed, Alice edited a manuscript by changing all *mays* to *cans*. Roger Fry's wife developed a thickening of the skull and went slowly mad. Modernism emerging, the war ten years off; Cezanne, from Aix, writes, "I progress very slowly, for nature reveals herself to me in very complex ways."

On the way home from grade school I cut through the woods and fashioned myself an actual crown of thorns out of a dead vine. I told others I'd been commanded to wear the crown by Our Lady who'd appeared to me in a grotto. That no one believed me was not a surprise. For some reason "grotto" struck my sister as hilarious.

Likewise, the stigmata turned out to be "Gardener's Triangles" which happen to women under stress. So only in my dreams am I among the female saints, strewing rose petals as I did in processions, bleeding. In actuality I am teaching this course which involves a series of poses: modernism emerging, emerging, emergencying, emigrating, elongating...

Here's one way to read this: like connect the dots, go from disfigurement to disfigurement. From my chin to Aunt May's eye socket, the grotesquely full to the grotesquely empty. In

between Stein's poem on milk, Tom Eliot dining with V &
Leonard, she says his face is like grim marble. Some vortices
I wish were still around, I tell my students, might include all
this belief in images, imagining perfume on a dress that makes
me so digress.

My first husband remarked that despite my disfigurement I
had a softness of skin that distinguished me from others. It is
a fact that one can't experience one's own skin. When pregnant, though, I enjoyed lying on my back and scraping my
nails over my belly. They left little red streets of insidious
intent that faded in a minute. I wrote messages on my
husband's back, hate and love, which he'd guess correctly. I
loved the skin of my babies, the difference between behind-
the-ear skin and back-of-the-neck skin and skin on the bottom or knees. All of it lovely, creamy, delicious but distinguishable as butter is distinguishable from silk. The skin on
boiled milk is famously repugnant as is, for some, peach skin
with its fuzz. In my refrigerator are apples whose skin has
shriveled, one banana with a black skin, and the slimy skin of
mushrooms two weeks old. The skin of dogs is unknown to
most as is the skin of most other mammals. It is a fact that
one can't experience one's own skin except through the pro-
nouncements of a lover.

"I paint forms as I think them, not as I see them," said Picasso
and I share this quotation with my students, as I do Pound's
poem "In a Station of the Metro." We are halfway through
the semester and modernism continues to emerge. Pound composed "Metro" after noting faces in the Paris subway, one
more luminous than the next. Picasso beat women, Pound

committed acts of high treason. The face in the modern crowd melts into an atmosphere of neon greed or is it yellow angles with noses? My students melt into an atmosphere of clanking heating vents and the world outside the window which is snowing a late spring snow that clings to branches as, in another season, time, country, petals cling to wet black boughs.

I could make much of the fact that my father stopped looking at me. In my face he saw the unrevisable, a poorly constructed sentence decreed by God. Also, I reminded him of his younger brother who died at 18. What is it that draws the eye or repels it might be the question formulated to explore these issues. On my grandmother's front porch in Coventry, Connecticut, my sister and I swung on the green porch swing while nearby our Aunt May stared benignly at a tree. There was the world framing her: the tree with its blossoms, the far away lake with its slither of blue sky. There was Aunt May framing the world.

A few years ago when I consulted a plastic surgeon for a precancerous growth on the side of my nose, she told me she could fix my chin quite easily. A slice and a tuck is how she put it. An office visit. It's hard for me to imagine my face without the flaw of chin scar. What had been empty would now be full. An eye in Aunt May's eye socket staring eerily out. Who would I be? My father, now dead, would swivel his eyes in my direction. In Picasso's famous reworked painting *Les Demoiselles d'Avignon*, the viewer has been eliminated, making "voyeurs of us all."

Therefore, with my scarred chin, as if from birth I'd been cursed with two original sins, one removable, the other indelible, I trudged through the woods on my way home from school. In the sky a cloud seemed to gather up and assume a shape that I wanted to be a vision. I knelt before it, knowing its falseness. Making the crown of thorns becomes, then, a punishment for being unworthy of an apparition. I wanted to tell everyone this as they waited, six or seven grade-schoolers, on the sidewalk where the woods path ended. I prayed for an apparition and wound up making myself a crown of thorns which tangled in my hair. My father laughed when my mother told him this story. I listened from the stairway, seeing them between the painted spokes of the bannister, heads bowed over dinner. I wanted to tell them everything, but I had not yet emerged.

HAPPY
GIRL

Somewhere a happy girl is walking. On Willow Avenue. Her feet ensconced in Mary Janes. Her hair in formidable bangs.

Curtain rises. Happy girl walking. Tree trunks are shaking their leafy leaves. Nowhere a breeze like this. Nowhere quite like this, says Martha, the happy girl, to her companion.

The fields are awash with something like light. You can almost see the cups and saucers streaming through, says the happy girl.

The happy girl's life is perfect. She has a boyfriend and three charge cards. Above her the leafy leaves twirl and hum.

I never knew about the sound of the world until this minute, until this minute with my shell-like ear tuned to the click of Mary Janes on the grainy pavement where so often I broke my mother's back.

Listening to jazz, the sound of a trombone, for example, the haunted drill of it into the air of the room. Happy girl at home now. Companion on a chair in front of the fireplace. What is it you were saying about the feel of the air? he asks.

I was walking along, this must have been childhood, only not so painful. The other kids disliked me. I had a haughtiness which I've worked hard to banish. Haughtiness banished, she proceeded to live her happy life.

What else can we say about her? She broke her mother's back countless times, not without guilt. Each crack. Her mother had been ill. In a wheelchair. She positioned herself by the telephone, writing in a crabbed script, little notes to people whose relatives had passed on. In the morning she prayed to St. Anne, patron saint of _____. The happy girl no longer remembers who St. Anne was the patron saint of.

But she remembers the forsythia. Which were yellow. A long tube of them fluttering around the hand.

Do you remember when we kissed? he asks. It was without tongues, nevertheless soulful. Your lips slid over mine and I felt the tip of your tongue and your mouth opened slightly. It was a very nice kiss, I thought. Little did I know it would be the last one.

Was this the last kiss you ever kissed? He didn't ask her this but continued with his bored somewhat amused demeanor to gaze into the fire. Any minute he would leave and just knowing that made her anxious. When would he leave? When would he leave? Sometimes she thought she would die without him. Then when he left she would eat something, occasionally an entire pound of spaghetti with leftover sauce.

But she was a happy girl, as aforementioned. She wore a smile and always had something cheerful to say to passersby. How's the soup? Nice shirt! Etc.

Her mother, she whose back had been (metaphorically) broken by the happy girl, never wept, though lord knows she had reason to. She sat in her electric wheelchair which sounded like a sewing machine and buzzed through the house straightening up. A piece of lint, a framed photograph askew, the wrinkled arm of the slipcover. Why don't you comb those bangs, she would suggest to her daughter who was already failing in her happiness. Why don't you wear a nice pin?

She was already failing in her happiness, that is to say, she was beginning to notice a rift between her happy aspect and her inner life which resembled a gnarled and ancient tree trunk.

The leafy leaves.

I'm happy if you're happy, he said. I only want your total and complete happiness and will do anything to procure it. He didn't say this.

When she analyzed her feelings about him she realized that what kept her in thrall was very superficial. She thought him extraordinarily handsome. She regretted his sexual problem, which they never discussed. He would not sleep with her. He was content to hover by her fireplace and eat her chips. Her pistachio nuts. Drink her imported beer.

This mainly irritated her.

In a comparison of this companion with her mother, she discovered they had certain things in common. Their fastidiousness, their hair color, their way of looking at her with a combination of fondness and dismay.

Often she walked alone. The world was so enormous above her, she kept her head screwed into the collar of her brown coat. She disliked her clothes which seemed to have nothing to do with her. At this moment, though, she was thankful for them. The largeness of the world, which accentuated her own tininess, her very insignificant insignificance, hovered above with its misshapen clouds.

You think your life sucks, he said. He had a way of speaking that made her regret her fondness for him. A bald, thoughtless, unnuanced way of expressing himself. If only he would take off his clothes, she often thought.

Was she or was she not a happy girl? How does one measure happiness? Is it in the eye of the beholder, like beauty? Is it? Is it? Everyone thought she was happy. They elected her to office. They telephoned frequently. She had no desire to see anyone but him and to engage in that special, uninspired talk which was their specialty together.

You have green eyes, he informed her. This she knew. He

touched her cheek with a fake fingernail. He was on his way to the bathroom. Can I stay here forever? he asked her. No, she said.

Then she told him that she was thinking about not only the feel of the air, how hard it was to express, like the taste of something acrid, like onions, but also she was thinking about death. Not affection but death, she said. On her arms were a cluster of little red dots which a doctor informed her was due to a low platelet count. These are hemorrhages, he, the doctor, had said. He had been unusually cheerful and unworried so she supposed she shouldn't worry, but here they were, these red dots which were actually, according to the doctor, small explosions beneath the skin. Blood, he had said.

What if I die, will you go through my journals? she asked him. It never occurred to me, he said, only now that you mention it, I might.

Often her mother would telephone. Her mother's voice had become cracked with age. She could hear the little catch in it hundreds of miles away through the telephone wire. She could hear the age in her mother's aging voice and the sparrows chirping in the vicinity. In the vicinity of the mother which was a room with green wall-to-wall carpeting and several pieces of furniture covered with the same floral fabric. Sparrows nearby, probably outside the mother's window, in a tree, or were they in the mother's voice, as the voice faded and these small chirping noises took over. Perhaps the chirping sparrow noises were not the noises of sparrows but something that invades the body at a certain time of life, the time of life that is closest to dying. As the voice fades and cracks. The leafy leaves in the tree humming.

I'm bored, he announces. I'm bored with everything in my life. Are you bored with me? she doesn't ask him this.

But he is beautiful and his beauty reminds her of that time of forsythia, the long yellow wand of them and their beaten blooms. Reminds her of her hand reaching out to them, of the tearing motion of her hand on the stalk and the greenness inside. If he leaves, so too greenness.

Happy is as happy does. She cleans her cupboards with him watching. His feet up, trying on her sunglasses, her new velvet hat. She thinks to give him a pot and a wooden spoon to bang with, as if he were an infant. You are an infant, she says. Seeing herself then, her terrible fondness for him playing across her face the way in the desert the wind will blow across and dismantle a few things.

So too her life. Happy and not happy. Existing in a kind of wave, which rolls and diminishes. Dismantled.

Stacking the white cups, cleaning the white shelf, replacing the old paper with the new viney one, seeking solace in the curved, cupped shadows, his perfect nose, bitten fingernails, the marvelous and the non, whatever happens. Which is the way it appears to her, happiness, its arches and ebbs, its miseries and singed winds.

Whatever happens, I will be happy, it is my new resolve, says

Martha to her companion, who is frowning steadily at something, an ant or beetle crossing his knee. Did you hear me? I said I will continue to trundle on, I said this too shall pass, I said hand me those scissors. And she sees him, ridiculous and permeated by grief, his round eyes aswirl with guile as he hands her the scissors by their gleamy eyes.

And the light washes in and out and the leaves make a noise that sounds like whoosh whoosh ah! through the screen and the jays are bashing their wings, yak yak yak, like the flutter of her heart in its cage, like her happiness flying away.

FAMISHED

I try to keep track of things but often forget what I've just made a mental note to keep track of. In malls across America everyone looks purposeful, no one seems to be wandering around without a destination in mind. My shrink asks me after every session where I'm going and I say I don't know and he is delighted by this answer, as if I've managed to circumvent some pressing life requirement. Once he said, "I think I'll try that."

When I'm depressed I make fudge. Without measuring I pour in sugar, Hershey's chocolate, milk, stir for three and a half minutes, ease in a lump of unsalted butter and burn my tongue tasting. Pain and pleasure rolled into one exquisite activity. I savor that little blister at my tongue's tip until it vanishes, then I savor its ghost.

The thought of sending Christmas cards is unbearable to me but I am a fabulous shopper. Today I bought fruit-scented soaps imbedded with triangles of colored glycerine, a navy blue rubber shirt, grey sweatpants, and a neck sachet. Yesterday it was ceramic mugs with cute representations of cats, a nail varnish called "plum pudding," and fused glass earrings.

A month ago I met a married man who wound up becoming my lover for one evening. He had the biggest penis I'd ever seen and because I wanted him to, he masturbated as I looked on. Afterwards I felt incapable of intimacy and when he telephoned I hung up on him.

My first adulterous affair was with a drummer who took me to a loft in Greenwich Village, set up a screen of blank stretched canvases around the single bed, and screwed me six times in a period of four hours. Outside our canvas "room" his pal the saxophone player practiced renditions of "A Train." When I confessed to my then-husband he purchased a how-to manual for lovemaking and held it in one hand while he positioned my legs with the other. I never saw the drummer again though I once wrote a poem about him called "V-Shaped Moment."

On Sundays in my town, many including me can be found at a diner called Bill and Nada's. Among the attractions of this establishment are paper placemats with pictures and vital statistics of the U.S. presidents, business cards available at the cash register with photos of Bill—dark-framed glasses, plastered hair—and Nada—beehived, lipsticked—from about thirty years ago, and the Brains and Eggs special. I am happiest sitting in a vinyl booth with the various elements of my breakfast arranged in front of me: toast, eggs, bacon, coffee, small juice, extra butter pat, tub o' jam. Nearby people read newspapers or talk to their partners across the tables. Lovers

are here, fresh from bed, tousled, shining, disappointed, eva-
sive, greedy, bored. I put a quarter in the table jukebox and
play Otis Redding and wolf down my food with a violence
that causes me to contemplate myself: a piggish, famished,
unlovable woman with grimy fingernails. She must be alone.

PARADISE

Once, on an airplane, a woman stumbled into the aisle seat next to my window seat, sobbing. She opened a large fabric handbag, took out a stack of letters tied with blue yarn, ripped them into pieces of paper, shoved the ripped paper into a vomit bag which she stuffed into the elasticized pocket in front of her. The yarn she wound around her forefinger. My fucking life sucks, she said, wiping her nose on her sleeve.

Another time I rode a prop plane next to an Arizona prison guard. He looked about 19, slight, crew cut, smallish tattoo of an anchor and a rose above his wrist. He believed in the death penalty and to illustrate its wisdom told me all about X, a death row inmate who'd killed two inmates and vowed to kill a guard. Literally uncontainable, X had sliced his way out of double-thick plexiglas enclosures countless times and was known to make zip-guns from screws in a matter of seconds. The screw would become the bullet, sharpened on the cement floor, the guard said. He'd kill anyone. It must be because he's claustrophobic, I said. He must be crazy. He must be a genius. The guard had long bony fingers, almost delicate, and a little smirk on his mouth, which was also delicate, thin. I imagined him being raped repeatedly, smirking, his uniform pants around his knees. Would you care for my peanuts? I asked him.

An airline pilot passenger who was stuck in the jump seat took the empty space beside me. He drew me a picture of wind shear on a yellow legal pad. First a cloud, i.e. weather system, then a series of lines coming down and curving up in all directions to indicate the wily path of the wind. A plane was then placed, in blue ballpoint, at the outermost tip of the wind-wave, and the pilot said, *That would be it.* Although I didn't fully understand, I was not anxious to know more.

My worst moment of flying comes when I picture myself on earth gazing up at a tiny silver plane. That would be me at this moment, I think, light-headed at the image of myself hurtling through space. Being in two places—the place of awe (looking up) and the place of dread (inside the plane)—at the same time.

The woman who tore her love letters into shreds told me a complicated story of a boyfriend who dumped her, but she was crying because her father was dying, not that she got along with her father. He was dying in Boston and gathered at his bedside were his estranged wife, her mother, and a sibling she had never met. She also owned seventeen cats and showed me a photograph of each which she kept in an album in the handbag.

The pilot had Tourette's. He twitched throughout the three-hour flight, knee smacking into his food tray and upsetting Cranapple cocktail, arm jerking out to slap mine at irregular intervals. I read Baudelaire: *Folly and Error, Avarice and Vice/ Employ our souls and waste our bodies force.* Why did you underline "black masses?" asked the pilot, twitching.

The sobbing woman wore a nubby green sweater, low-heeled pumps. The pilot wore a grey suit, top shirt button undone, brown tie untied, cuffs unfastened. The prison guard wore a white tee shirt that had seen many washings, silky black hair on his wrists beneath the tattoo and beneath the knuckles of his long, bony fingers which you could imagine strangling a neck.

The pilot thought I was a satanist and took out a tiny New Testament over which he crouched, twitching. The sobbing woman, dry-eyed now, recited her employment history: first education, then ed-admin, then corporate, very good at corporate, then moved in with boyfriend, quit corporate, backed boyfriend's recording studio. I have my whole life ahead of me, she said. Clean slate.

The little square plane window holds always, remarkably, the same view: part of a wing, part of a cloud, a section of blue. Always the same though the proportions may vary, wing as foreground, cloud as theme, sky as punctuation. Or vice versa.

The pilot made a list of safe and unsafe planes. He said: Avoid two-engine planes when traveling overseas. I told him about my scariest flight when the pilot announced he had drifted off course, flight attendants handing out free booze to every-one, regardless of age. Eleven-year-olds drinking miniature bottles of scotch in preparation for death.

The criminal called X sliced through the double-sided plexiglas in a matter of minutes. Although the guards wear bulletproof vests beneath their shirts, the screw-fashioned bullets are able to pierce them. It costs thirty-thousand dollars a year to keep an inmate on death row, the guard informed me in the man-ner of one who has repeated this sentence thirty-thousand times.

I love to fly. I love the compartmentalized food, I love the window seat, I love the restroom with its murky light and the rules about smoking, flushing, and returning to my seat. I love the seatbelts, their fat shiny locks, their durable nylon straps and the way the food trays flip down and rest on my knees and the headphones and the button which causes the seatback to drop exactly two inches. I love the orange oxygen masks with their terrifying apparatuses and the comforting knowledge that the seat cushions can be used as flotation devices. I love *SkyWest* magazine, the white credit card phones and the fact that for x amount of time, my job is to sit here and kill time. I love being between places, and so nowhere, en route—it feels to me like dreaming.

On a flight from London to New York an eighty-year-old Iranian woman begged the pilot to allow her to sit with him in the cockpit. Amazingly, he agreed. The flight attendant es-corted her up the aisle, through the plush and redolent first class section and into the utilitarian pilot's quarters where she was strapped into a bucket seat in front of a large, curved windshield. Oh, it was so beautiful, she said later. She had been on her way to visit her daughter who lay unconscious in a United States hospital, and she said it was like flying into heaven, into paradise.

PRINCESS

1. Eventually she would wake up. Her soul roosting like a little bird.

She would wake to a world whose clouds had vanished. On the stove something simmered in a pot. Her hand fluttered to her neck, fingered the filigreed pendant with the single diamond. *The sky is high, the Emperor is far away.*

2. I am lying on the hard ground in Massachusetts, twilight, the few green blades of grass poke up stiffly, as if dead. He's on top, fully clothed, tongue in my mouth, grinding himself in. He fingers my filigreed nipple with the single diamond. What does it matter how the sky looks with its few insipid stars?

When she awakens it is as if to the same world, deceived by the light. On the stove a familiar hissing, a familiar, insistent hissing. In minutes, the Prince will come on his camel, his feet enclosed in wheel-pins, *sabatos* with spurs, kiss or not kiss her.

3. The refugees huddle against one another crossing the border. It's hard to believe this is real life and not a troop of movie actors pretending to be us at our moments of crisis. If you close your eyes, a dream is waiting there in the darkness. Open them and the sky is not lit up with flame or smoke, but calmly looking down at the docudrama of our lives starring Ben Gazzara and Suzanne Pleshette.

4. She will eventually awaken to the sound of a seven-piece orchestra composed of tri-horns, Uzis, fodder from B-52s, shattering bricks, rocketing china, burning, tumbling bodies—a slow sizzle fading on the way down. Suzanne Pleshette, playing the god-mother, enters stage left.

        In my memory there was rigid grass, greyed by a kind of half-light; his penis through his jeans felt sharp, rocking in between, even through all our clothes. My blouse was white with buttons. The ends of his fingers square, blunt-edged. He fingered the blunt tips of my nipples, like lug nuts, he said. Like diamonds. Eventually he died in a car crash, too fast, drunk.

5. Led by Ben Gazzara, the refugees cross the border. Eventually we will have to go back, says one man. But in the meantime they have gotten us to sign papers saying we are KLA and now when we return there is no record of our citizenship. Imagine the refugees encased in a 27" screen, walking, stumbling, gazing at the camera. We are tragic, they say into the mouth of the camera, into the teeth of the camera.

        The image of tragedy is different from its heart, says the Prince, looking sadly into her eyes, she who eventually awakens, whose hair flattened into the disintegrating linen of the pillowcase has turned, in the intervening years, grey.

6. *The sky is high, the Emperor is far away.* This popular Chinese saying evokes a buoyant atmosphere of freedom. When the Emperor is away, one may surmise that constriction has vacated the earth. The Princess awakes, the Prince returns with his lips, Suzanne Pleshette and Ben Gazzara are oddly ennobled though miscast. I'm wallowing in the middle, between longing and liberty, the Emperor and the TV show, the Prince and the car crash.

7. I hardly knew him when he died, years later. It was in Florida. Lights blazing, his neck thrown at an odd angle, thin legs through his jeans very still like branches snapped from a tree at the moment of impact.

   We can see only so far into our futures, says a Holocaust survivor, an ethnic Albanian refugee, an Iraqi prisoner of war. And this is not fiction. There is suffering and the story of suffering, two different things, says the Prince. But I'm still in love with you, she says, awakening. Eventually, she would not be.

ISLAND
TIME

When I was a young bride I lived on an island in the Caribbean. One day I was married in a fashionable suburb of New York—it was June, raining, a portent—and the next I flew to the island where I would spend the next five years of my life. As we came in for a landing, I remember thinking the water looked like a sheet of taffeta, the same color as my bridesmaids' dresses. I was twenty-one years old.

Even at twenty-five my husband was what we called a "soldier of fortune." He'd already traveled around the world on Greek merchant ships and had been chased by the ship's chef with a knife. He wore a green Brazilian fertility symbol called a *fega* around his neck and had only recently (in honor of the wedding) shaved off his beard which had been burly and reddish, a mark of his bohemian, adventurous character. I suppose this is why I fell in love with him.

We lived in a tiny apartment over a garage on the other side of the island. To get there required a long drive through the mountains. Picture it as a kind of gigantic pie with all the apples mounded in the middle, and the sides where the cities and the coast were tapering down flat.

It made me seasick to drive through the mountains. The road was narrow and dangerous and studded with a number of hand-fashioned crosses where people had inadvertently driven off cliffs. The mountains were bright green and too close to the car, rising sharply and garishly on either side of us, making me dizzy. There were always cows grazing on the steep rises, and once in a while a little band of goats or a man walking with a staff, his head in a bandana. Through the tangled foliage peered the every-which-way outlines of shacks with roofs made out of old planks or corrugated tin. I tried to imagine life amid all that green, situated in a landscape where everything seemed tilted, living in a shack, tending the cows and goats, but I couldn't put myself there.

They breed special cows in these parts, joked my husband, their inner legs shorter than their outer legs, and at first I believed him.

I believed everything and I believed nothing. My life had come to a peculiar pass where nothing surprised me and where, at the same time, nothing mattered. Minutes after the wedding ceremony I'd felt a sinking in my stomach and I knew then that my marriage was doomed and that we were fated to watch the doom unravel to its sad conclusion.

The garage apartment we lived in belonged to an old couple who lived in the large square white house below us. If we stood on our concrete balcony we could see through their windows at night. They'd be eating supper in their undershirts, sitting on plastic lawn furniture around their dining room table. They were quite elderly and tiny. I was from a

class of people that would never eat dinner in their underwear and so I was charmed by this practice and also by the
plastic chairs which bespoke the otherworldly attitude toward
material goods I'd thought of cultivating, especially when our
wedding gifts arrived. There were so many crates I felt
ashamed. Also there was no place to put anything.

We stacked the crates on the patio and prayed it wouldn't
rain. Eventually, my husband built shelves on the walls of the
tiny living room and I did my best to arrange the gifts on
them—silver chafing dishes, cocktail shakers, Waterford crys-
tal, toaster ovens. There was something useless and absurd
about these items, even then, beaming down on us from those
plywood shelves, which probably led to my abuse of them
through the years.

My husband was a drinker. Sometimes he drank whole
bottles of hard liquor—scotch or gin—and then he'd pass out,
snoring horribly throughout the night. He didn't drink every
night, but when he did drink, he went on until he collapsed
or until the bottle was empty, whichever came first. One night,
after a party, he hoisted himself to the end of our four-poster
bed and urinated loudly on the floor. Other times he simply
disappeared for a few days, leaving me to concoct a story for
the neighbors. I had a strong sense of propriety which, as
time went on, eroded magnificently. But in those days, his
disappearances embarrassed me, confirming my failure as a
wife.

During one of these episodes I read *Madame Bovary*. I
can still see myself, legs up on a green plastic chair, sun pouring on Flaubert's amazing pages. *Madame Bovary, c'est moi*,
Flaubert is supposed to have said. But I felt *I* was Emma
Bovary, vain, dreamy, hopelessly trapped.

Like Emma, I'd been educated by nuns in a convent school, I'd had high hopes and then married a man who fell short of my dreams. That Emma was adored and I was not would seem to be our main point of difference, but this never crossed my mind. No, what I fastened onto there on the concrete porch as my knees turned bright pink in the tropical sun was our yearning—mine and Emma's—for something better to occur in our lives and the awful feeling that this was too much to ask.

* * *

Many years later I am teaching *Madame Bovary* to a class of 50 or so university undergraduates. The novel begins with Bovary's absurd multidimensional hat. The hat—whale-boned, felt, pelted, stitched, equipped with "lozenges of velvet and rabbit's fur" was "a head-gear of composite order," Flaubert tells us, "one of those wretched things whose mute hideousness suggests unplumbed depths, like an idiot's face." In fact, I tell my students, the hat is almost impossible to visualize, whereas the idiot's face is not. I'm getting at how the modern novel, like the hat, involves impossible issues of representation. What do you make of this? I'm always asking.

My students say they liked Charles better than Emma. I poll them: two to one in favor of the poor husband, the poor deceived husband. Most think Emma is a bitch. A healthy minority think she is "a victim of history." A few admire her and wish they could be her, without the death at the end.

On their initial encounter, Charles notices Emma's hands— "not pretty"—and fingers surprising him with "the whiteness of her fingernails." Suggesting what? Vanity? Sloth? Pride? A character flaw makes its first appearance on page 17: "She could not find her workbox."

I always bit my nails, though not in the usual way. I'd tear them, beginning at the edge, across and down. Sometimes they'd bleed in the corners and a stiff little prong stuck up I'd have to grip with my teeth and pull as if a weed. Slovenly, my mother said of me even though, during the ceremony, as opposed to the marriage itself, I looked nice in my Balanciaga gown, a gold cross tantalizing my cleavage. *C'est moi*, I thought later, wanting what? To be adored.

Outside grimy snow crowds the windows, the ventilation system, the metal shutters. There's a tapping noise from the radiator. The girl with nose rings has a question. Why *c'est moi*?

*   *   *

There was nothing special about my husband's co-worker Mike Dean. He was short and even a bit tubby. He might have been the blandest man I ever knew: the same beige color hair and skin and eyes and he wore tan-framed glasses. But he had a serious bent I appreciated—unlike my husband, he was resolutely without jokes and double entendres. He had a bookshelf stocked with self-improvement books, and he didn't drink. At times I caught him glancing my way almost furtively, twisting his fingers on his lap or shredding up a cocktail napkin. I imagined he was in love with me and this felt like salvation, just knowing that someone could be.

We became a threesome, eating our meals together, traveling to the coast together for the weekends. We even shared bedrooms with Mike Dean; he'd throw his sleeping bag on the floor of our hotel room and pay half the price. In the mornings, sunlight blazed through the filmy drapes of wherever we were and we'd head off anywhere—to breakfast at one of the drowsy cafes by the ocean or to the plunging ocean itself, where we'd race to catch the first good wave. Being a threesome balanced us out; my husband's hangover spirits improved and I wasn't so mopey.

My husband was everything Mike Dean was not—hardhearted, unreliable, brave. My brothers still tell the story of how, years later, they watched him emerge from our Connecticut home in his three-piece suit, ready for his commute to work. Jacket over arm, he strode to the side of the road, tore off a long branch of flowering dogwood, re-entered the house and emerged once more in shirtsleeves with his fishing pole. He was handsome as a movie star—Robert Redford or the young Michael Caine—and he did whatever he pleased.

Eventually, Mike Dean declared his love for me. We'd been sitting in a cocktail lounge and he reached for my hand and held it a while. It was not as thrilling as I expected. But it was a comfort and so I left my hand in his for the space of an hour. Who knows if my husband noticed? He himself was given to flirtation and, as I said, he was a drinker. Also, it was not the type of thing he would have noticed. He was obsessive about conversation and tended to black out the world when he was on a subject that took his interest, and he was holding forth that night. It was balmy under the island palms and we were drinking concoctions with rum and juice and the music was playing from a neon jukebox. I sat with my hand in Mike Dean's, not daring to move a muscle, thinking of Emma and Leon, Emma and Rodolphe, thinking of disappointment and death and perfidious women whose ranks I would soon join. After an hour, I removed my hand. It was sopping wet.

In the end, I was only mildly flattered by Mike Dean's attention. I had to admit to myself that the man I loved was the man I married even if it was painfully obvious he did not feel the same. Not that he loved anyone else, not that he ever loved anyone at all. But I was twenty-one and I believed his failure to love me was about my unworthiness to be loved. Now he was discussing the benefits of cigarette smoking (he worked for a cigarette company) and he held our table of friends in thrall, not because the subject was interesting, but because he was insistent. If a head would dare to turn or an eye carelessly wander, he'd call them back to attention by aiming his remarks aggressively their way. It's an effective trick, one he probably picked up at the Dale Carnegie school he'd attended the previous summer.

So while he lectured on the charcoal filters of Lark cigarettes, which all of us smoked anyway (I still remember their peculiar taste, like a pot roast injected with formaldehyde), I left my hand in Mike Dean's, suspecting gloomily that I'd finally found my lackluster correlative. Later my husband staggered off to the golf course with a friend, each waving a bottle and laughing too loudly, like ugly Americans. I sat with Mike Dean who was too shy to say anything much, which was fine by me. I used the time to gaze into the night, at the dark figure of my husband off in the distance and to wonder, like Emma, when my time would come. For what? For anything.

But the island was beautiful, like a fairy tale beginning to a marriage that proceeded backwards from its promises into more and more trouble and misery. To pass time, I played golf with Mrs. O'Neil. She was a wife of one of the Commonwealth Oil people who were stationed on the island. She had short, over-permed hair the color of whole wheat bread and in all the months we played golf, making our way over the hill and dale of an irregularly kempt golf course, she never asked me to call her by her first name. I remember most vividly a time when a troop of speckled cows came lumbering over a rise on the 8th hole and chased us into a field. The cows were angry, their nostrils flaring, Mrs. O'Neil was tearful and not a very good runner and I rolled in the field and laughed until I choked. Because it was ridiculous, Mrs. O'Neil with her Kleenexes, the cows with their pulsing nostrils, this island with its scraggly palms and tiny jabbering inhabitants, our apartment with the pitted tile floor, and my husband who barely looked at me anymore. Also, I was pregnant.

*   *   *

Flaubert said that in *Madame Bovary* he was trying to get at the color of the wood-louse, a certain shade of greyish-brown, which I imagine inconsequential, therefore possessing an appealing subtlety. In 1852, he wrote to his lover, Louise Colet: "You speak about a woman's sufferings: I am in the midst of them. You will see that I have had to descend deeply into the well of feelings. If my book is good, it will gently caress many a feminine wound; more than one woman will smile as she recognizes herself in it. Oh, I'll be well acquainted with what they go through, poor unsung souls! And with the secret sadness that oozes from them, like moss on the walls of their provincial backyards."

I imagine also the wood-louse, like the human woman of a certain era, is one who burrows in, camouflages as it feeds, a little ashamed. The moss on the other hand is a romantic trope for "secret sadness," which is undermined, even pathologized by "oozing," which brings to mind wounds and danger, not to mention yeasty secretions and period blood. Gross, says one of the boys in the back row, the one who usually sleeps.

*　*　*

When Emma had her baby girl, she suffered immensely from postpartum depression. When I had my baby girl, it was like falling in love for the first time. For hours I'd gaze at her face, so perfect in a way that amazed me, and my mind was empty except for euphoria which, far from the color of a woodlouse, was like the island as I'd imagined it, all full of blue and breezes and sunlight. Her tiny fingers would grasp my gold-hooped earring and tug and even then, my eyes tearing with pain, I'd gently rub the inside of her wrist until she gave up. For a while she slept between us in our double bed, but I was always afraid my husband would roll over and crush her so I put her in a bassinette close by.

Mike Dean was no longer in the picture. He had faded away as meekly as he'd appeared, this time to somewhere in the midwest for another job. My husband became less and less interested in his job. He developed a malady called Dengue Fever which kept him in bed for hours at a time, sweating. In between bouts of this disease, which he caught from a mosquito, he drank scotch. Once or twice he hit me.

You can imagine the rest of the story. You'll be glad to know that I left finally with my four children, escaping into the night in a borrowed VW bug and all our winter clothes even though it was summer. Already this story is leaking in another story, one I don't care to recount right now. It is years later and what I yearn for is the island itself and the feeling of hope it gave me. I would sit with my baby on my lap and she would nurse from my breasts as the waves rolled in with their frothy lips. She would wind her fingers around a loop of my hair or she would blink at the big long-legged cranes that marched along the shore leaving footprints like Japanese line drawings.

Or do I yearn to be choked with love once more, like Emma, needing the drug of herself in the eyes of another? She could not find her workbox; she pricked her finger and sucked her own blood like a vampire; she despised her husband, ran up the grocery bills, fucked her way once or twice into a kind of happiness. *C'est moi*, said Flaubert. Me too.

Though it's a miracle to have come all this way, from there to here—to scroll my way back to that time on the island when my husband drilled holes for our wedding present bookshelves, his blond hair falling heartbreakingly across one eye. Then, for a moment, I am who I was then, full of sadness, full of faith.

Meanwhile, the sleeping boy in the back row has opened his eyes and, in the front, the girl with the ponytail is asking another long question and I am writing on the board, chalk squeaking, giving us chills.

THE WOMAN
WHO LOVED
PETUNIAS

We were in the movie theater when a man in the back row stood up and shouted something. There were only about twenty people in the entire theater. We were watching a movie about a guy who went to the city—New York—in order to make a new life. He had a black roommate and was on the verge of getting a new girlfriend. It was an artfully done movie, full of amber light and talented actors no one had heard of. All of us liked the feel of the movie and were distressed when the man shouted. I turned to Debby and said, What did he say? I'm occasionally hard of hearing, but I gathered that whatever he said was unfriendly. Debby said he said, *Women always get their way*. I shuddered. A chauvinist in the back row didn't bode well for our movie. Also, he seemed drunk.

It was not long after when another of us, Sharon, decided to leave the theater. She pushed across Debby and me and raced up the aisle. What's going on? I wanted to know. Sharon had gone to get the manager because the man was crawling around on the floor in back of our row of seats, drunk as a skunk.

So the rest of us, Debby, Pam, and I, left too. For a while I stood in the back of the theater, reluctant to abandon the man in New York City and the new Italian girlfriend who was very intellectual. I'm intrigued by these fairly recent portrayals of intellectual women as desirable. It seems like a step forward.

While some are fueled by indignation, I like to like things. I see this as neither vice nor virtue, but rather as a way of surviving, of feeling confident about the world. For example, I tended to give the fellow on the floor the benefit of a doubt. I imagined him heartbroken, drunk, therefore harmless but suffering. Likewise, it gave me a particular pleasure to see the movie hero shun the fluffy blonds in their miniskirts and go for the plainer, but plainly more interesting, dark girl.

Eventually we got our money back and were told the police had been summoned for the drunk man. Everyone was afraid to go near him; he was acting too crazy, mumbling biblical passages and, according to Debby, shouting his police badge ID number out to the world at large. He's a cop and cops have guns, she reminded us wisely.

We were in the car at that point, Sharon's fancy Acura. I was looking for a car myself, something plusher than my two-door Nissan. Through an unfortunate circumstance, I had come to a turning in my life: my daughter had been in a motorcycle accident and was trying to recover from a severe brain injury. For the past two years, I'd taken care of her. As a reward, I found myself yearning for convenience and luxury. I wanted leather seats and power steering and automatic transmission. I wanted a big house with built-in bookcases and a few charming but functional fireplaces and a garden. Probably I didn't want any of these things badly enough, though, since I kept putting off my car search. These days everything was moving a little too fast.

I had only recently returned to Tucson after a five-year absence and unlike most stories of return, I felt nothing had changed. Here I was with my cronies at the movies, for example, and if anything had changed at all it was only that one didn't worry so much in the old days about some nut in a public place. But that was true everywhere.

So instead of the movie, we went to a bar and ordered champagne and oysters. A tall blond with an earring waited on us and seemed amused at our high spirits. Above us, the tiny recessed lighting looked like stars. I didn't talk much. I had the sensation, possibly champagne-induced, that I was luxuriating in the sounds of my friends' voices, their stories, and even their beautiful presences, swaddled as they were in silk and velvet and linen, all wearing fabulous shoes and carrying fashionable purses. I'm not so sure how it happened that Debby came away with an etched bottle of a certain brand of gin, but I think the waiter must have given it to her.

These, as I've said, were old friends—friends from a former life—and although I felt nothing had changed among us, there was something in their very indifference to time that struck me as odd. I felt as though I'd traveled a long way only to return to where I had been before and when we talked, I felt both of the group and outside of the group. About that evening, there had been a dreamy, underwater quality and I had the brief sensation that my friends were actually exotic tropical fish, preening, dipping, and swaying. Sharon wore a red velvet shirt with a pointy seventies collar and Pam was gorgeous in some kind of dark silk. Debby, the only one of the three whom I was not close to before, was vivacious and funny. With ease she quipped with the waiters and bartender and I found myself envying her way with people. I was aware that my envy was tinged with nostalgia. For hadn't I once been easy and vivacious myself? Still, I was not uneasy that night, exactly, just removed. Not even uncomfortable, but content to settle back and enjoy, as if I were watching a TV show or an aquarium or even, come to think of it, the continuation of the movie about Ed.

The oysters were mouthwatering—though not perhaps as luscious as my current memory of them—and the champagne delicious. I found myself getting a bit tipsy. At one point Sharon leaned over her champagne glass and told us a story and it is this story that I want to tell here, since it has stayed with me for some weeks, and I think that telling a story—or, as in this case, retelling it—will bring to the surface its lesson, though I'm not sure a lesson is exactly what I mean.

The Woman Who Loved Petunias

It was October and though the leaves don't change in this part of the country (since there are few deciduous trees), there are subtle changes that the long-term resident recognizes. Through the warm air, one feels in the beginning of October little needles of coolness, the sky's blue deepens, the ground softens. And there are other changes—almost imperceptible: the curling of a zinnia leaf, the paling of a bloom, the doves' summer stridency calmed to a little chorus of mumbles in the branches of the palo verde.

That day, overhead, a large white cloud sailed by and cast, for an hour or two, a glum oblong shadow in the swimming pool. It was time, Pam thought, to buy flowers for the garden. She visualized petunias on either side of the front door, near where a stone lion bared its fangs and where there were now only grey, reedy leftovers of portulaca. She tested the soil with her fingers. Tepid, like a baby's bath.

On the way to Western Garden, she allowed her mind to play over possibilities. A crop of red penstemon by the tamarisk, a dizzy spin of globe mallow by the lion; then petunias in all colors everywhere else, for their smell and for their papery frailness. She was a woman who loved petunias. They reminded her of old, fragrant women with cheeks as transparent as tissue, so ethereal they might suddenly dissolve in the air. But petunias, like old women, are resilient; they bend and flex in the sudden Tucson gusts—they fold up like handkerchiefs, then flap open to exhibit their little stoical hearts.

In Western Garden she wandered among the beds in a reverie. How wonderful to be just this person on just this day, just this woman who loves petunias and now has the capability of purchasing them for her garden. Ahead of her, a man pushed an oversized plant cart with a boy on it. The boy was sitting down and holding onto the sides of a big pot of blue hydrangea. A woman like herself—middle-aged, nicely dressed, wearing crisp gold earrings—stooped to inspect a rose. Beyond the bedded plants were row upon row of trees, bottle brush, acacia, California pepper, palo verde, mesquite. This is where she was now, walking among desert trees on narrow pebbled paths, on her way to the petunias, whose smell she could detect coming closer, in sweet gusts that to her were never cloying, but friendly, calming.

She chose all colors, as was her plan: white, pink, dark purple, peach, lavender. She loaded fifteen flats onto her cart. Already they resembled a garden. The sun was passing behind another cloud, the second voluminous cloud of the day, when she heard a loud clap. Thunder, she was sure of it. She looked into the sky, at the white cloud shaped like an old-fashioned automobile, which had covered the sun halfway. But it must be thunder, with lightning soon to follow, for here were people racing by: two women, one of whom was she who had sniffed the rose not five minutes ago—she caught the tiny glint of her earrings as they sped by; the man with the oversized cart had swooped the boy into his arms and was running toward the parking lot, leaving the hydrangea and his cartload of plants in the middle of a pathway.

In the desert, people acted strangely in storms, all out of proportion to the actual danger posed, though Pam had recently seen a newspaper article about a blind and deaf man who'd been struck by lightning and regained his faculties. But to regain one's faculties could be dangerous—she pictured the man, stunned by vision, stunned by sound, disoriented, lost. How much of our lives is our inflexible version of it?

Just then a person with a nose ring stumbled into her, almost knocking her over. Quick, run—there's a man with a gun shooting people! These were her words delivered in a frantic, breathless voice, and Pam understood them perfectly. She repeated their fantastic gist to herself: man with gun, shooting people. Still, she could not bring herself to run to her car. For one thing, she had chosen her petunias. She had chosen them with care and she had hauled, well, shifted, fifteen flats of them onto her cart. And for another she was still in a reverie, a dreamy, inchoate state of mind that had begun with October's needles of coolness and fixed itself in the oblong shadow in the swimming pool and in a longing for flowers, namely petunias. Also, within her deepest soul, she knew her time had not yet come.

Therefore, rather than running for her car, she squatted and watched for the gunman from behind a hedge of petunias of all colors. People, the one or two still left in the gardens, pattered by quickly; she heard the sound of their feet along the pebbled paths; then silence as clear as a lake, she could almost see to the bottom of it. It was in the silence that she felt her heart beating fast and hard. A fly buzzed nervously around her head and she was afraid, suddenly, to swat it away. Another shot rang out, she heard it clearly this time, not thunder which was a complex, nuanced sound with tonal variations and unpredictability, but gunshot, mechanical, flat. Where was the gunman?

Truth be told, there was a part of her that didn't believe in the gunman. An unreasonable part, to be sure, because in the distance she made out the shape of someone wearing a ban-dana, red and white, the kind she used to wear around her head when she jogged. But she wore it as a sweatband and he—she presumed this was the gunman—wore it more fash-ionably, covering the head and tied above the back of the neck in a wing nut knot.

Then she heard the sound of someone weeping, and the gun-man ran toward her holding his gun, she could make it out clearly now, a chrome and black lump in his hand, his hand which waved it, then finally hurled it where it landed not far from where she squatted behind her petunias. Then the weep-ing gunman (for it was the gunman who wept) lept over a wall; his leap was so graceful, like a dancer or a tiger, one fluid motion of arm and leg and torso, and he was gone.

She doesn't remember how long she squatted there behind the petunias, taking in their scent, as if it were a drug. She recalls the look of the gun on the pebbled path, near a rack of begonia. So dead-looking, she thought, like a corpse itself. She considered retrieving it; she was curious about its weight and heft. She imagined herself walking toward the Western Garden parking lot holding the gun away from her body but pointed somewhere (for a gun had to point somewhere!) and what if it went off? And what about fingerprints? No, she would not retrieve the gun.

When she finally stood, she realized she was trembling so much she could hardly walk. She made her unsteady way to the parking lot of Western Garden where a man lay dying on the concrete— the dark patch oozing beneath his body looked exactly like oil dripping from a car. A woman with long, dark hair who cradled his head in her blue-jeaned lap, whispered softly to him as if he were a baby.

Later, in the newspapers, she read that the gunman had shot two people, both employees of Western Garden and that he himself had been a disgruntled employee—this is the phrase the newspapers used: disgruntled employee.

In the end, of course, she left her petunias behind. There would be no petunias this year, she decided, because how could she plant them now?

Now that I've recounted the story, I can't see much of a lesson. Anything can happen—maybe that's the lesson. Maybe the lesson is to be on guard every second, to keep in mind that a gunman or an insane person in a movie theater or a life-changing motorcycle accident could happen at any time and for no reason whatsoever. Or maybe the lesson has to do with the perverse concept of sacrifice—no petunias as a tribute to the murdered people, instead of fifteen flats of them planted throughout a garden, giving pleasure. Or a dubious sacrifice: giving up a movie while some drunken, probably harmless slob wallows in sorrow and humiliation. Or any number of sacrifices that a person might make in order to continue to live—or in order to continue to live as the person one wants to be.

That night I was tired. I'd had a good time seeing my friends, but now I wanted it to be over. I'd left my 26-year-old daughter, Dotty, with a sitter. She'd miss me, I knew. She'd need me to angle her wheelchair to the right position alongside her bed, to flip on the brakes, so that in the middle of the night she could transfer safely into the chair and make her way to the bathroom. She'd need me to lie beside her and stroke her face and hair and answer the questions she couldn't seem to remember the answers to—rudimentary questions like *what happened to me? where did we go today? what year is it?* Without those answers, she'd be lying there in the darkness, literally and figuratively, with nothing to hold on to.

So what are you going to do about Dotty? Pam asked me suddenly. The question made me uneasy. I'd been taking each day as it came; I didn't have a real plan. But Sharon, Pam, and Debby had become solemn; I felt them converge upon me in their luscious silks and velvets, their eyes eager and sharp. Then the room itself darkened, as if a cloud had eclipsed the tiny star-like lighting. In another world, Ed was betrothed to his Italian girlfriend, the man from the movie theater was sobbing on a couch, the woman who loved petunias was turning on the TV, trees were rustling, the wind was blowing, the real stars were spinning in their orbits, in various shades of brightness.

TUTTI
FRUTTI

1. A blue Ford and a highway with a stripe down the middle. Mountains curving and receding. Who has the wheels? The girl's name is Roseann. My name is Paul. I have the wheels.

2. How many times have I shoved into fifth gear, downshifted into fourth, then third, while leaning into a soft curve, soft as the shoulders of Roseann? Wasn't there a song once called "Roseann"? I ask Roseann. But she is asleep, dreaming of Elvis. I am making curves like the paths of marshmallow on devil's food cake. Like where heaven used to be in the eye of Roseann looking into my own eyes which are brown. Brown curves, then. A grey day, a blue Ford and Roseann.

3. In her sleep, I have to admit Roseann is unbearably sweet, her shiny face pressed into the speckled upholstery of this Ford and even her little shoe, so *stirring*, aslant on her foot, or not aslant so much as half off and bobbing a very slight bit so that there is a moving shadow on the floor mat.

4. And in my anxiety to be faithful to the appearance, an exact rendition of Roseann's shoe, dropping or rather dripping from her foot, held on it seems only by the strength of one small big toe, in my intention to represent this with some amount of exactness, I almost crash into a truck. Our car swerves and Roseann herself, sweet unruffled Roseann, even she gives a little yelp, like a puppy. Oh, my puppy, I say. And she re-closes her eyes and continues her dream about Elvis.

5. Elvis is mounting a large staircase whose bannister is made of gold. He is wearing a spangled shirt with some silly fringe around the collar and some gold jewelry, a necklace or so, hanging under the shirt against his moderately hairy chest.

6. Questions for historians: Did E have a hairy chest? Did he have corns? A large penis? A hairpiece?

7. We are on our way to the Church of Elvis, did I say that? This is Roseann's idea of romance, the Church of Elvis and me, Paul, aka the guy who won the Elvis look-alike at the Coons County Fairgrounds. Otherwise I'm a grade school teacher at Wasatch Elementary. That's in Salt Lake. I'm a fair grade school teacher but an excellent Elvis impersonator. However, and this is a sad fact, I do not like Elvis and so my impersonations are tinged with contempt. Not that Roseann notices, being herself completely devoid of an ironic cast of mind. And being in love with Elvis. You read about people in love with famous dead stars but you never believe they are for real until you meet one. In my case, Roseann. I do not love her—she is not intelligent and this gives all our interactions a kind of rueful simplicity which wears thin. I do lust

after her, her sweet toes, the silky slope of her shoulder, the bath-oil smell of her armpits, cheap I'm sure, but intoxicating nonetheless. Her mouth.

8. Elvis is pulling off a cowboy boot. Now he moves, one-booted, to the stove where he gazes with some deliberation at the electric burners. Above his head, a noisy mobile of cutlery twirls. It reminds him of a song. Or a hound dog.

9. Sing to me Paulie, Roseann says. We are in moderate traffic, hemmed in by semis, sirens off to one side. My reward for the Elvis look-alike was a fifty-dollar gift certificate to Jud's Boot Hall. At Roseann's insistence, I purchased a black shirt with sequins stitched across the chest and pearls on the cuffs (the boots begin at $150). I do not care for it. My style is somber, I'd like to think, classic. Oxford shirts. A tie of perhaps silk with a pert emblem repeated along its length. Love me tender, I croon, though my heart isn't in it.

10. At Wasatch Elementary my students sit in neat rows of eight across. At row five there is a break which makes an aisle. I have never been able to understand why this break comes at aisle five and not, more logically, at aisle four. It requires that I jog a bit to the left before entering the aisle and performing my duties. Children, I call them. Which they resent. They turn up their palms for my inspection. Grubby little hands, often smeared with the remains of a meal. Peanut butter and jelly, most likely, or a little ripple of grease, as from an abundance of mayonnaise. Of course, their nails are revolting, imbedded with filth, as if about to sprout radishes, as my mother used to say.

11. Roseann has rolled down the window of our blue Ford and is trailing her hand in the air like a child. If it weren't for her sweet twat I would chastise her severely for this behavior, which is dangerous and foolhardy. Up ahead the semis float nearer and nearer to one another and it occurs to a part of my mind that they will smack into one another and that the smack will create a terrific series of sparks. In this same part of my mind, I am able to view with perfect clarity the astonished expression frozen on each driver's face, the rivulets of blood trickling...

12. In Roseann's dream of Elvis she has entered his kitchen wearing only her slip. Elvis is flipping pancakes wearing only one boot.

13. I am driving Roseann to the Church of Elvis which is located in Memphis, Tennessee, across the street from a Texaco station that sells memorabilia as well as gas. Sixty miles into the trip, Roseann wants to stop. I really have to take a leak, she says. She reaches under her tee shirt and unbuckles her bra. From the corner of my eye, I believe I see her scratching her boobells. I call them boobells since they are quite voluminous. I am very sweaty and hot in this car, she says. I had no idea you didn't have AC.

14. I have known Roseann for thirteen hours. We met at the Elvis look-alike contest at the Coons County Fairgrounds. She was the one sitting in the first row smoking a clove cigarette. After my performance, she offered me a blow job. After the blow job she complimented me on my large penis (thank you very much) and suggested we visit the Church of Elvis.

What the hey, I said. She is not an intelligent woman by any stretch of the imagination but she has lovely, smooth skin, as my mother would say, and tremendous boobells which I enjoy streudling.

15. Elvis flips fourteen pancakes. Roseann leans against the counter in her slip. Through the kitchen window the paperboy may be viewed on his bicycle. He tosses the paper onto the front stoop. Roseann raises the hem of her slip very slowly. Elvis is pouring syrup. More butter, says Roseann.

16. It is no longer twilight. I am getting a headache due to the bathroom beseechments of Roseann, now rising to a bitter pitch. I have told her repeatedly that it is not permitted to stop. Here, I want to tell her, whipping out my very large penis, suck this. Take ahold of this here in that little rosebud mouth of yours. My puppy, I would add, as an affectionate touch.

17. The moon is a fuzzy smudge in the sky. The sky reminds me of the construction paper the children at Wasatch Elementary use to fashion their incredibly clumsy masks, involving glue. Which brings to mind Roseann's dream of Elvis slathering butter on the pancakes and elsewhere.

18. Of course, I do not say any of these things to Roseann. In America, I tell my students at the Wasatch Elementary school, we are not required to say what we think. Stick to observable facts, historical facts, scientific facts, I tell them. The Mediterranean is a sea. The Titanic was a ship. George W. Bush is our president. Salt Lake is our city. Elvis may or may not be

interred in a white mausoleum that sits at the end of a garden amphitheater in Tennessee, an amphitheater—*so Roman! Imagine the gladiators!*—surrounded by thick, plantation-style columns and filled with an ocean of beribboned bouquets, giant teddy bears, heart-shaped candy boxes, all of which foreground a round, blue-as-an-eye swimming pool adorned with a black fountain and two ice-cream-cone-shaped yew trees. In America, I tell my students, Elvis is king, regardless of his whereabouts.

ON
VISION

It was obviously in December. Snow flurries were predicted, but at the time it was raining in long lines recollecting arrows or spears. We wouldn't have described ourselves as happy. Always going forth into the night; always in search of the perfect woman or tableau, as in a group of youths shouldering one another beneath a lamppost. Their shining faces put us in mind of something evanescent Heidegger might have construed. *Dasein* as opposed to *Weltsmerz*. Two women sitting at a round table at Quo Vadis, fur muffs slung evilly over chair backs. This would only be the beginning.

One leaned forward, the other leaned forward, their round heads making what we heard to be a splatting sound. Mouths snapping open and shut as shreds of flesh and plant matter disappeared therein, eyeballs bulging beneath thick lids smeared with colored grease, in this case blue-green. Which is when what Georg Simmel said about the human face occurred to us—"considered from a purely formal perspective," he said, "it is aesthetically unbearable." How right he was!

In those days, it was our misfortune to be a photographer, to go among the uglies, recording them for posterity. We owned a Hasselblad 400 single lens and a wide-format Polaroid, hard to come by in those days, the kind employed by Lucas Samaras. Under normal circumstance, we used the Rolleiflex with twin arc lamps, of a kind of low infrared preferred by Avedon since we too were portraitists.

Our rooms were sheeted many times.

We had an eye, as they say, and in the window glass it roved around trying to stuff the city into its bag.

After we inherited a million dollars we also bought a palm-sized 35mm Nikon and a 35mm Canon Sure Shot which was not much of a challenge, but occasionally required for thematics. Thematics were important. We bought some black clothing for thematics.

We kept careful watch at night because we'd read the predictions. Sometimes a gang of boys racing through a yellow pool of artificial light stirred a wind behind our eyes. The sidewalk shimmer made their faces float and we itched to get at them.

We were artists. Our rooms were sheeted variously and from time to time a client came to call. We were not hospitable, we knew this. We offered tea. We kept the toilet brushed. The client removed her clothes and posed against the sheets, taking up required postures.

Thematics were important and we preferred that which we could dispose of easily.

Heidegger: "No thing corresponds to the word and meaning 'being'."

Freud: "The alternative—either-or—cannot be expressed in dreams in any way whatever."

Blake: "This Earth breeds not our happiness."

Our philosophy was a particular view of the city in which we contained ourselves. When Freud theorized about dreams, was this not a way of reminiscence? To recollect—*re-collect*—his daily aimlessness into coherence or, more likely, to make formula of his crimes. The windows of the city, surrounded with stone decoration, occasionally a gargoyle glowering guilelessly, were portents of the eyes behind them, hovering above chairs or plates of food.

The woman next door had red hair swept up in a chignon and kept in place with a lacquered stick. She owned a black kitten which deposited two clumps of brown vomit on our doormat. We owned a black book with red corners in which we'd keep track of insults to our person or possessions, it amounted to the same, according to Locke. This woman's name—Suzanne—had appeared many times in our book, as well as her cat. Cat vomit, aforementioned. We owned a cat who was grey and lifeless through no fault of our own. We frequently had a wind behind our eyes that sharpened into rings of neon surrounding each thing in our range of vision. Still, nevertheless, we kept our rooms sheeted. The client would enter carrying an amber-colored umbrella which she would rest against the hall wall.

We waited for snow to obliterate the city's grime and filth. We sat at the window ledge, craning our neck to see the clouds which were black and low-slung and positioned in a curious, malevolent way. On the streets, silence and spikes pervaded. A dog walked by, its head dangling in front of its collar, as if choked; a woman in a dirty raincoat was casting around for an address, checking a yellow scrap of paper, rotating her head at particular intervals which could only be the intervals between buildings. Her neck made a sound like an air conditioner, a loud whir with a glitch in it and we had an impulse to call down to her. Eventually she would arrive at our door with her umbrella and her confusion.

Our cat crawled out of hiding and spun himself around the table leg in order to inspect her. She was thin as a rail and her face held a neurasthenic pallor. She was not cooperative, but we tried, we tried our best. Behind our eyes an irritable wind came up.

Her raincoat was the color of ashes and from a ripped pocket seam a cluster of threads protruded like a splayed foot. Her fingernails were bitten past the fleshy lids of her fingers and along one nail bed was a line of dried blood; her eyes were a dull green and very extremely staring so that right away we knew we'd have to employ the thematics.

Blake: "Thought chang'd the infinite to a serpent."

Heidegger: "The infinite *no longer* manifests what the verb otherwise reveals."

D. Donald Peat: "A man riding in the dream of his cat is infinitely unknowable."

We kept our library sheeted during business hours. The client removed her sweater, her yellow blouse, her brassiere, as instructed. We set up the arc lamps and aimed the Rolleiflex here and there. There was a humming coming from somewhere, distinctly annoying.

Question: Is our neighbor practicing her violin during business hours?

We recalled the story of the women's arms found in the dumpster that morning.

Our rooms were sheeted in order to avoid the intermingling of our business with our personal lives.

We had been raised in the country where cats and mice freely sauntered, but this was not a time of liberation.

The woman threw back her head and smiled at us slyly. She reminded us of a rat we'd seen once in the gutter outside the building, squatting down next to the curb, almost invisible in the greyness of the concrete, who fixed us in its eye beam, producing a sly smile much like the client's. It crossed our mind to imagine her without arms. Then, before we knew it, she was putting on her clothes.

"We weren't really finished," we said.

"I have no intention of fucking you," she said, surprisingly because that thought had never crossed our mind.

"Who'd want to fuck you?" we retorted.

In our mind's eye we saw the women's arms coming apart so easily from her shoulders, as if there were no bone at all, just meat, very soft and red. The women in Quo Vadis also sprang to mind, as one was carving a lamb chop and talking with her mouth full. We were raised in the country and so stories of meat and slaughter do not really shock us. The previous day, a man had walked by with three cages full of violent, squawking parakeets, so you see it was everywhere.

Question: Why did she leave before we were finished?

Outside it had begun to snow, *enfin*. From the window ledge, we watched her go, her dirty raincoat catching a film of vanishing snow. The wind had come up quite unbearably behind our eyes and there came a point when we could no longer watch her making her pathetic way down the street, not bothering to raise her umbrella.

For Blake this and other moments partook of the eternal, the woman's form not unlike the abject forms in *Plate 11 from Europe*—limp, collapsed body, distorted, miserable face.

We had an urge to express ourselves, to go further into some representation of snow slipping sideways or buildings buttressing balconies, or blankness, which is what snow—*snow!*—created around us in those moments, like a fallout of words covering our dreams.

Like a fallout of words covering our dreams, we kept our rooms sheeted and our cat, who was grey and lifeless through no fault of our own, slinked around our peripheries with infinite sorrow.

The word "infinite" keeps reappearing—casually slung, overdetermined—regardless of its failure to acknowledge history and progress.

Question: Was Blake's city with its low, grim buildings, its cobbles, spilled slops, injured horses, lice-infested amputees, so different from our own?

We imagine the sky during a snowstorm and the sky during a snowstorm remains a constant blanket culled from a fixed menu of appropriate options. Also, around this time of day—six or seven p.m., the woman having hurried away with her rudeness and her amber umbrella—we cannot help but picture the other woman, the one who might at that moment be marching armless into the dizzying landscape, like some sort of victor or saint.

D. Donald Peat: "Behold my soul with its false look of horror!"

The great millennial philosopher might just as well have said "look of false horror," because what is "a look" if not a play of words around the face, like black plastic poked through with holes?

After a light supper, we swept the floor. Crumbs and various strands of hair, an amount of torn-up newspaper and junk mail, dust which had formed itself into bitter lumps, pennies. Through the thin walls we heard our neighbor Suzanne admonishing her cat, the TV making a pleasant din which suddenly seemed emblematic of that millennium. Nevertheless, I noted the insult to my person, the voice of Suzanne with its syrupy, cloying edges and the image of the cat it called to mind, covered with vomit or shit.

We closed our black notebook with the red corners. The wind behind our eyes had faded to a breeze peppered with a few spiky whiffs of what would come to pass sooner than any of us predicted. At the time, we were thankful for the simplicity of our lives, for our meal which consisted of two slices of rye toast and an egg, for our little flat with its street-gazing windows, and for the city itself which had begun to shake uncontrollably and wail like a newborn.

THE SOUL
IN ITS FLIGHT

1

She'd been dreaming about a woman who lost her memory and when she woke up she thought she *was* that woman, but then she recognized everything in the room: her own underwear draped over the floral chaise, the picture of palm trees in the brown frame, as well as the familiar scraping sound of the snowplow up the drive. Her head ached between the eyes and farther up on the crown of the head and when she moved from side to side a throb blinked on and off spasmodically, like some thwarted neon sign blinking sadly at midnight over the unobtrusive and only partially successful Time Market owned by the family down the street. The man's name was Roy and he was fond of her. He spoke in an ebulliently inflected voice. "Hel*lo!*" he'd say. "How *are* you? Why we not see you these *days?*" dragging out the 'a' in 'days' and pronouncing the 's' as if it were a 'z' so that the word sounded slightly sexual or at least insinuating and jazzy. He annoyed her profoundly. He wore a baseball cap frontwards and was tall and in addition to the few paltry food items—hard-cooked eggs, stalks of celery, soda—he also rented out videos of the worst sort.

It was morning and she'd not slept well and now she was thinking of a man she hardly knew, a man who annoyed her even though she hardly knew him. How unfair! she thought suddenly. She was given to self-accusation, to obsessive intro-spection, to daily renewals in the form of fervent promises she would invariably break.

She sat up in bed and grappled for her glasses on the bureau next to her bed. The bureau also held a broken digital travel clock, a photo of herself and her daughter, arm in arm, wherein she looked quite robust and heavier than usual but terribly young and carefree. Her daughter, on the other hand, looked pallid, wearing a blue and white striped outfit and smiling thinly as though she'd been coerced to pose adoringly with her mother. Also on the bureau: a bottle of brown Obi nail polish, a starfish, some stainless steel toenail clippers on a ball chain.

Through the chink in the heavy beige drape provided by the condo owners, a little sliver of white sky hovered near the porch railing. It made her think of the cat made of fog in T.S. Eliot's famous poem. She never wished she were dead because the idea of committing suicide was repellent to her, but that morning she wouldn't have minded being dead instead of alive. There was a difference, she felt, in wishing for death and not caring one way or another. Her own father had just died, not even a month ago, and she felt that his passing had made familiar some territory that had hitherto been daunting and unimaginable. Since his death she fancied she heard him mumbling in a greyish afterworld, his voice rising and falling incoherently, but recognizably. No doubt this incoherence was a matter of her own inadequacy, her failure to "hear" precisely that other world, and not a difficulty with her father's enunciation. She felt he was trying to tell her something, but not something especially important. She felt that he was chattering compulsively instead of meaningfully. Very distinctly she felt, this morning of the dull headache, that he was a bit bored, that he missed them all, and that, as in his real life, he was still checking up on everyone, only now he had less power to effect changes in their lives. This last fact made her terribly sad, for her father had been one who could always effect change, if only by raising his voice a decibel and directing its volume here or there. Yes, this is the way in which he'd effected change. He'd been a powerful man, for better or worse, and it was inconceivable to her that his energy should ever leave the world. Which apparently it hadn't.

Her daughter was still asleep under the purple duvet in her room. She had the habit of sleeping in on the weekends and her mother liked to let her sleep most of the time—only today she wished that someone were awake besides herself since she felt unnaturally alone and even a little frightened. Physical illness, such as the headache, made her think of mental instability, of nervous breakdowns and scenes like those in Olivia de Havilland's *Snake Pit*, of women clawing at walls and/or rocking in chairs, scratching and talking madly among themselves.

To calm herself, she read for a while in the numerology book, which assured her that her number for the year was 6, a service number, but a number with great rewards, and that her LIFE ESSENCE-DESTINY was a 4 or 9 depending on which name she chose to call herself, which was always more complicated than it should have been because of two ex-husbands, a pen name (she'd published a few poems) and a maiden name which she'd despised for many years since it was the name of the father who tried to control her life. Taking back her maiden name after her two divorces would have given him some pleasure, she'd always imagined, so she'd of course refused to do it. Now that he was dead and she was feeling in the region of her heart an unstoppable ache for the loss of him, her only father after all, who'd supplied half the DNA for her being, and whose admonishing phone conversations she longed for beyond all reason, she again considered changing her name back to the original, but such a decision seemed hopelessly skewed by sentimentality and therefore untrustworthy. Also, it was only fair that she should be deprived a name she'd selfishly refused before. She was in the habit of meting out her own punishments for sins, a tactic which she felt appeased the Almighty, if there were an Almighty.

She hadn't been to confession for years, but when she imagined going again she saw herself proclaiming a litany of general faults rather than particular sins: SELFISHNESS! AVARICE! LUST! PRIDE! she would shout to the priest, denouncing herself rigorously. She was less willing to provide the specific narratives, which were matters of shame to her. This was the reason she'd left the Church to begin with: she felt its curiosity was prurient. Once a confession priest asked: "Did he put his hand under your bodkin?" and she said she didn't know what a bodkin was. Was it, "When he himself might his quietus make/ With a bare bodkin," as in Hamlet, a dagger unsheathed? Or was it some incredible article of clothing, an undergarment with straps and hooks? Still, if she'd continued to confess, then maybe she'd not have been so obsessively self-judging. There was that confession phenomenon: when you left you felt cleansed. You saw the soul the way the nuns drew it for you: round and incandescently white, like a light bulb glowing and pulsing in some obscure part of your anatomy, prodding you forth.

The father had died very suddenly. He tripped over a sneaker and broke his hip. Then, during surgery, complications set in. His heart failed, his lungs went into shock, and he had a stroke. Still, he managed to hang on long enough for his four children, now in the worrisome grip of middle age themselves, to gather around his deathbed and disconnect his life supports in accordance with his living will. Then, for forty-five minutes, they watched him die, mainly by watching the monitors over his bed, the speeding and then slowing of the heart rate, the speeding then slowing of respiration. Then death. The lights were low in the intensive care cubicle. The light, she thought, since she'd also acquired the distressing habit of translating her surroundings into metaphors, had been the color of urine. She'd cast around for this analogy and found it handily in the catheter bag dangling from the side of his bed. She sent a mental telegraph to her father. *This is the room in which you'll die.* How extraordinary to end a long life in a room so dim and ignominious. Every once in a while a male nurse who looked like a teenager came in, solicitous, asking if he could do anything.

Also on the bed table were three white, translucent stones given to her by her friend Barbara. They were the size of robin's eggs, collected from dunes around the Pacific coast, in Mexico. Barbara had given stones to all her friends and to her she'd given the three white ones. They weren't smooth like river stones but slightly textured to the palm and one had a fissure in it when held up to the light, sort of a brownish line, and behind that was a darker irregular shape, so that it appeared a bug fossil had been trapped.

Living in this condo under rumpled sheets, gazing through chinks in the heavy draperies at a sky which seemed feline in its hovering by the porch railing, she was aware of getting older. Year after year piled up like the bills, accumulated like a collection of hats on a top closet shelf—fedora, cloche, base-ball, straw—so that together in a dark clump, they lost their distinctiveness. She, too, seemed to be melting into the earth from whence she came, acquiring (like hats) new wrinkles and little pouches as her face "surrendered to gravity"; and her ears and nose, as she'd been warned, were becoming per-ceptibly elongated. A shape asserting itself around the hips threatened their symmetry and her memory was not good. On the wane, too, was her eyesight which in the past had been a matter of some pride to her and now, without her glasses, the world was a distant, unapproachable blur. A ghost.

Also on the night table was a tiny carving of the Buddha. It was red and purchased, she believed (for the daughter had purchased it), at The Dollar Store. The surface of the night table was a map of her psyche to be deciphered or at least acknowledged. The Buddha, the stones, the nail clippers.

Things strewn randomly but, like the I Ching, producing significance, given the moment and the light. The fog that nuzzled the windowpane like a cat, etc.

She thought she might like to paint her toenails brown, but her hand was not to be trusted at this hour of the day. It shook. It twitched. The grocery man had noticed it. "Why your hand-a shake?" he'd asked her once, by way of making a joke. "You have disease?" he inquired heartily. "Ha ha." She tried to ignore him but he was very loud, he spoke loudly, and when she frequented his shop (which was only in emergencies these days) he assaulted her everywhere—by the ice cream freezer, by the video display. "No more cigarettes?" he asked her. "You still write poetry?" His curiosity about her was perverse. He liked to watch her squirm and shy away, she felt.

Dear Mary, she wrote on a card which depicted one Botticelli angel entwined with another, *Thank you for your nice note* (crossed out) *sympathy in regard to* (crossed out), period. *It's been a long time.* There she paused, remembering Mary as she'd been during college, her brown, shiny, very straight hair and her large grey-blue eyes. She pictured her very clearly, standing in a plaid skirt and wearing knee socks. She wondered what she wore these days. Indian print skirts and long sweaters? Birkenstocks? She had been a girl you could imagine growing into that kind of woman. She'd had an arty bent and was overly serious, perhaps a little humorless. In her note she'd said she'd never married and had never had children. Not that this, in itself, was proof of anything, one way or another. Her mind drifted off, its channel changed. A bowl of pears on a polished wooden surface. A still life superimposed on the mind's far wall. Mary had a been a painter, but whether she painted still lives or something else, she had no recollection. She was still in bed with her pen poised over the note card. But she had drifted off. *Thank you for your sympathy. It's been a long time* was as far as she got. She could not even bring herself to reiterate the fact of her father's death. Tears sprang to her eyes through which she saw the room's accoutrements suddenly alive and shifting, perhaps in the act of vacating the room for some other, more habitable space.

The daughter sauntered in with a toothbrush in her mouth. "Jar a vera fa," she said. "I have no idea what you're saying," said her mother, impatient. "Take the toothbrush out of your mouth or don't say anything." "Uh oo," said the daughter angrily, slamming the door on her way out of the room. The mother and the daughter had, actually, a quite good relationship, which entailed being able to say what they wanted to one another. At the moment, the mother understood the daughter as having said "Fuck you" and this didn't dismay her. Far from it, it brought her back to her senses, those senses that minutes before had been, she felt, in some kind of jeopardy. Things drifting out of the room, falling off ledges. Her father mumbling beneath it all.

He still mumbled. What did he want? "How are you?" she said out loud. "I can't stand not knowing," she said. The door opened. "Who are you talking to?" demanded the daughter. She wore an orange velour sweatshirt and some very baggy jeans. She was overweight, but had a lovely face. Freckles. Very expensively straight teeth. Hair, now that she thought of it, not unlike Mary's, though at the moment it was wet. She stood in the doorway with a blue bowl of cereal and a spoon, shoveling it in. "Can I use your blow drier?" she said.

The daughter had come to live with the mother after the last marriage was terminated. She'd thought she'd go to grad school, but something happened and she changed her mind. She moved in, then, and did not go to grad school. She took the back bedroom with the iron bed, the green sheets, the purple duvet. She had made several collages for the walls since, like Mary, she was an artist. The collages involved fabric from several of the mother's thrift shop discards and one silk kimono which the mother had not thought to discard. The collages were very good and had received praise. One was called "Summer Dress." Another was called "Folder." A third was called "My Mother's Kimono" and this one was the one made of the old kimono which the mother still wished she owned so that she could wear it on mornings like this. Mornings when a dark mood descended and lifted, descended and lifted, like someone running around perfectly fine, then the next minute a patient etherized upon a table, for no particular reason or for all the reason in the world, like today, a day not long after the death of her father.

In the kitchen she opened a green tin and nibbled on caramelized walnuts. It was all she could think of to eat. Her daughter was toasting bread and slathering it with apricot jam. The air was misty outside and she reasoned that, in such an atmosphere, ghosts might come to call. She sincerely hoped her father would not do anything so thoughtless. She had a friend whose mother, Myrna French, had promised to send a sign that all was well after she died, and the sign had been some magnetic letters rearranged on a refrigerator: MYRNA FRENCH DEAD. This did not comfort the friend who said it was not the kind of sign she had in mind. Someone else she knew was awakened in the middle of the night by a dearly departed tugging on her toe.

2

By coincidence, the kind of coincidence that only life can provide, she happened to be teaching James Joyce's "The Dead" to her Intro to Lit class. "The Dead" is a story situated at a holiday party in Ireland. It is snowing. A man called Gabriel arrives at his aunt's house with his wife Gretta. Gabriel is a plump, slightly fussy man who adores his wife, but there is an element of smugness in his adoration. Gretta is a seemingly contented young woman who, toward the end of the party, becomes entranced when she hears a certain song being sung. She becomes dreamy and preoccupied because the song makes her think of her dead childhood sweetheart, Michael Furey. In the end, Gabriel seems to have a revelation about Life. The students quarreled about it. "I don't think so," said Alyssa. "I think he was just as repressed at the end as he was at the beginning." "No," said Robert, "isn't it true that all his life he'd been grieving for his own dead mother?" "Tell us!" screamed the students. "Tell us what it means!" But what she thought she knew was no longer clear to her. She stood in front of the blackboard and closed her eyes. She saw it all— everything in Joyce's story. She saw the candelabrum on the long table and the browned goose being sliced by the thin silver blade and the snow's big fat wet flakes and the look of the little houses and their yellow lights; she saw Gabriel hold onto Gretta's arm—she was wearing a red coat with fur on the sleeves—and she saw them walking down a long path of snow and the snow falling on them and finally covering them up. Then she heard her father's voice. "Don't worry so much," he said very distinctly.

In her office the department chair was waiting with a card. He gave her a little half-hug and the card, which was signed by many people, some of whom were strangers to her. She thanked him. He nodded formally and exited her office, backing out. He was a nice man, exceedingly well-groomed and somewhat dour. He would have been a good funeral director; he had the ability to work his features in that specialized way that conveys sympathy but not an unseemly amount of sympathy. The office was a mess. Papers piled everywhere. Files stacked on top of files. Unopened mail. Brochures from book companies. Notifications of lectures, meetings, parties. She threw it all on the floor. She used the side of her arm and swiped at surfaces. Things landed sideways, papers spilled out of files, envelopes bent and twisted. She tore lengthwise through a few file folders which took a lot of strength and made her hands ache. There was a knock on her door. "Everything alright in there?" Was this, then, a nervous breakdown? If so, it wasn't as bad as she'd imagined. Actually, it was kind of a relief. She had an urge to continue in this irrational vein, but she foresaw its ultimate tedium. What she thought she knew was no longer clear to her. On the way home she had a long conversation with her father, during which she remembered certain atmospheres she thought she'd forgotten.

3

Green. The fluid of trees and sky. Birds plunged and flicked.
The sky churned up and weeping. The girl on her back looking at trees through the ridges of her knuckles. The mother
calling from the screened kitchen door. Flash of checkered
apron, yellow wall. On the table, a red plate of sandwiches.
The radio playing *Kiss me once and kiss me twice*. The mother
dancing by herself. Of what does she dream, the mother, dancing by herself in the yellow kitchen? There are placemats made
on a loom, big strands of white woven together with yellow.
When the toast pops the radio song begins again, *Kiss me
once*.

Outside it continues to rain, sounding as though its heart will
break. So rhythmic the breaking of a heart, rat-tatting on the
roof and through the leaves in a rush. Like a snare drum.
Though what did she know about snare drums? In the same
kitchen at twilight, the prismed light goes flat. The child banished from the room. She sees so clearly the hunch of her own
lost back climbing the stairs to the bedrooms, grubby hand
on bannister. Around her shoulders like bruises her father's
banishing voice. A fat plume of self-pity flattening like a blanket, tears and snot slithering on the raised fist.

She was a brat, she understands this now, narcissistic and
shrill. *Keep Your Voice Down. Stand Up Straight.* Her hair
fell into her eyes, she lost her barrettes as well as her gold
signet ring.

Now she dares to enumerate, after all these years, items bur-
ied in the backyard. A ring, a snapshot of an uncle, barrettes,

one gold, one silver, two charms from the bracelet, a green fountain pen, crayons, eraser, a drawing of a cat, a plastic horse, a shell with a penny inside it, a book about stamps, the real foot of a bird, a puppet head. She told him the intimate details as if he would understand, the furtive digging with a soupspoon and the prayer as she tumbled each thing into its wormy coffin. "I felt I was preserving something," she told him. Or making history, a kind of song. She told him as if from the great distance that now separated them, he could bring himself to forgive her. "Please," she heard him say. "Enough." He sounded tired, defeated, as if nothing anymore were of consequence. It occurred to her she was tormenting him still and so she shut up. But she could not bear to think of him in that twilight of souls milling on a grey plain. She wanted desperately to know. "Am I right or am I right?" she asked him and his voice sank into a torrent of other sounds that ran interference between them.

On the way home, she stopped at the Time Market for the first time in months to buy toothpaste. Roy was overjoyed to see her. Like the department chair, though less successfully, he composed his face into a mask of solemnity, took her hand in both of his, inclined his head. Out of the corner of her eye she spotted a magazine she might have wanted. "Your father," he said. "Yes," she said. "Dead." "I know," he said, looking as if he might weep. "I have heard about it. He was an old man?" "Pretty old," she said. "I see, I see." He shuffled his feet, looked deferentially at his shoes. She headed for the magazine whose cover girl had teeth like Mary from long ago: fat teeth with a charming space between the two front ones. This was the same Mary who pierced her ears with an ice cube, a sterilized needle, and a cork. There was no pain but afterwards the lobe swelled and festered. The same Mary whose photograph in the wedding album shows her in a pale blue seersucker suit, sunglasses, looking solemn.

After she was banished to the bedroom she made her dolls' beds in the dark. One doll, a brunette with glossy, acrylic hair, always slept in the nude. "It's like Dachau in here," her mother said once, equating the death camps with inappropriate nudity. She (the daughter) never understood the connection.

Her ears bled a little, then swelled up, but she persevered with pierced earrings. Years later she punched another couple of holes, but the infection was too much for her and she had to have three earrings surgically removed.

If an equation can be made with dolls, it would be that the one with dark hair is equal to half the sum of herself because, though smaller, better behaved. Her father also had a gold ring which he wore on his pinky and which, in her childhood dreams, she saw flashing at unexpected intervals. Once she turned the head of one of the dolls around on its neck so that it faced backwards like a witch. But they were glorious things, the dolls, and their random arrangement on her floor produced significance depending on the moment and the light.

At her father's bedside she'd massaged his feet—such beautiful feet, long, white, aristocratic. His toes so still on the sheet; one of the brothers clipped his toenails with such gentleness and care and attention, she began to cry. Her sister cleaned the inside of his mouth with a tiny green sponge attached to a stick, then patted him on the head. His eyelids fluttered and occasionally sprang open and darted wildly around. A nurse called Kathy seemed especially fond of him and addressed him in that baby way nurses have of speaking to the barely conscious, as if to be dying were developmentally the same as infancy.

"Where are you, Daddy?" she cried in the car, the windshield wipers beating off the seconds, bum-bum-bum. "Where are you?" She would never have said this in real life. She never betrayed her need for him. Venus in Aquarius, giving a prideful independence to a person. At home the daughter was shredding the purple duvet for another work of art. It was horrifying to recognize its pieces on the living room floor. The duvet was twenty years old (at least) and now it was gone. "Not gone, recycled," said the daughter, her fierce face bent over a pot of glue and a huge flap of unmounted canvas. "I will call it 'My Life' and it will be simply the duvet. Nothing else. Strips of purple that can't possibly add up."

Also on the night table: a globe of the world, a lace cloth, a bronze bust of a woman with a muscular back, a tarot card, Wite-Out. A pencil holder in the shape of a buffalo carved by a very old man in Tucson, Arizona, and painted pink and orange. The stones given to her by her friend Barbara seemed to have traded places with one another and when she looked at the photograph of her parents' wedding day she was compelled to say it lied.

Because whose parents were so glamorous? They are both smoking cigarettes. The mother inclines her head for a light. Her dark hair slopes down her cheek, eyes downcast, the Belgian lace of her wedding veil lies upon her hair like the snowy froth of a wave. The father sucks his cigarette like a movie star, from the side of his mouth. Pall Malls. They could be an advertisement, these two. He has already, even on the day of his marriage, that slight impatient tugging about his features, as if this small passion will not be enough for him, or as if it is already spent, the wedding night, the honeymoon in Cuba, rage already bubbling up, eyebrows ferocious, racing ahead of himself into the iron sleeves of his life. Still, each of their glossy heads, like dolls, youth brimming in the champagne glasses on the banquet table, the silver candle sticks, white roses, smoke frozen next to the father's head like ectoplasm, the ghost of then, them, camera angle and beholder. Banished and banisher. He has the handsome-gangster look.

Her entrance into the kitchen, the warm yellow light, the placemats' white weave, the plates of food, thick ham steaks with pineapple, string beans in a bowl. Being told "ham is not for children." But why? she wondered, the beginning of unreasonableness, the parents furious, but why? Some mannerism, some thing she could never get hold of. Her voice quality perhaps? Too much hair falling in her eyes? Forgetfulness? But why? Banished up the bannister. Grubby hands. Making her dolls' beds. The train whistle through the organdy drapes and the wallpaper: dusky blue with silver ribbons culminating in loopy bows. Her sister helping her to pack a suitcase for boarding school; her brother, unable to walk, scooting in a tiny straw chair.

If a gold signet ring were among the constellation of items found on her bureau, the daughter would no doubt pilfer it for an artwork. In miniature: "My Mother's First Tragedy" which would be the tragedy of the monogram itself, having been given a name she could not possibly live up to. She hid her face in the pillow. "It's like Dachau in here." But it was not like Dachau, but a 6 year, numerologically, where service would be demanded and sacrifice for the benefit of the family cheerfully offered. The duvet as an example. One purple life from another's. In college, the girl Mary slept in the nude and was once surprised by a nun who stood over her as she slept. Now Billie on the daughter's stereo singing "He's Funny That Way," changing genders as easily as socks. *Dear Mary, Thank you for your sympathy. I'm not much to look at, not much to see....*

One life, she believed, was much like another, racking up years like spider webs or sheets of paper, without distinction, falling on Alabama, stars, Billie sang. After all this time she understood it to be this way, which was why her sorrow shocked her. Suddenly she was again at her own wedding, the band playing "Stars Fell on Alabama" and she in her father's arms, her white dress a cloud of shiny satin on his sleeve. His flowered lapel, her lipstick. The points of her shoes touching near his. Some piano interval between them, a few notes plunked into the stirred air.

So Gabriel and Gretta walk arm in arm into the cold Irish night of snow, each in his and her own world. At dawn everything will have changed. Is the heart's revelation so crucial? she wondered. So earthshaking?

She'd had a difficult relationship with her father who was now dead. He found her unladylike, stubborn, too independent. She found him cruel. He found her careless, uncompliant, selfish, immoral. She found him unfair. She had not realized the beautiful texture of his hair until she smoothed it back from his forehead as he lay dying. At some point it had turned the brightest silver.

She would find the photograph on the floor of her closet and be convinced it was a sign that he was doing OK. He is standing near the ocean wearing a blue golf shirt, slacks, and glasses. Over his head, a flock of palms, a picket fence, a house with blue shutters. His hands are clasped behind his back and the glasses mean it was before the worst of the macular degeneration. A glimmer of a smile, though he may be merely squinting against the sun.

The question was, how much of all this will survive? Even that morning's light swelling cat-like on the railing of the porch beyond the sliding glass doors would never return, she knew, and if the items on her bureau—stones, pieces of paper with scrawled phone numbers, paper clips mixed up with earrings, a minuscule marbleized book in which she had written years ago, *Story idea: daughter talking to bigshot father in office (gold pinky ring??)*, barrettes, her favorite fortune cookie fortune—*You long to see the great pyramids of Egypt*—(because it foretold nothing, choosing instead to acknowledge yearning)—if all of this were arranged differently, would it produce a new significance depending on the moment and the light?